THE BOOK OF NEWCASTLE

First published in Great Britain in 2020 by Comma Press.
commapress.co.uk

Copyright © remains with the authors and Comma Press, 2020.

'Calling from Newcastle' was first published in *Newcastle Stories* (Comma Press, 2004). 'Tabs' was first published in *Newcastle Stories* (Comma Press, 2004).

The moral rights of the contributors to be identified as the authors of this Work have been asserted in accordance with the Copyright Designs and Patents Act 1988. The stories in this anthology are entirely works of fiction. The names, characters and incidents portrayed in them are entirely the work of the authors' imagination. Any resemblance to actual persons, living or dead, events, organisations or localities, is entirely coincidental. Any characters that appear, or claim to be based on real ones are intended to be entirely fictional. The opinions of the authors and the editors are not those of the publisher.

A CIP catalogue record of this book is available from the British Library.

ISBN: 1905583109
ISBN-13: 978-1-90558-310-2

The publisher gratefully acknowledges assistance from Arts Council England.

Printed and bound in England by Clays Ltd, Elcograf S.p.A

# THE BOOK OF NEWCASTLE

EDITED BY ANGELA READMAN
& ZOE TURNER

# Contents

| | |
|---|---|
| INTRODUCTION<br>Angela Readman | VII |
| CALLING FROM NEWCASTLE<br>Julia Darling | 1 |
| MAGPIES<br>Angela Readman | 9 |
| TABS<br>Sean O'Brien | 19 |
| THUNDER THURSDAY ON PEMBERTON GROVE<br>J. A. Mensah | 33 |
| LIVING ON PLANET CLACKY<br>Glynis Reed | 53 |
| THE HERE AND NOW<br>Margaret Wilkinson | 59 |
| BLOOD BROTHERS<br>Jessica Andrews | 73 |
| DUCK RACE<br>Crista Ermiya | 81 |
| LOFTBOY<br>Chrissie Glazebrook | 99 |
| EKOW ON TOWN MOOR<br>Degna Stone | 111 |
| ABOUT THE CONTRIBUTORS | 119 |

# Introduction

EACH CITY HOLDS A whole library of stories, with some that are yet to be told. When it comes to Newcastle upon Tyne, the structure of the city seems to tell us a story about the people who have lived here through the years. The stones of the city walls tell us tales of medieval fears of invasion, while the city centre tells more recent, optimistic stories of prosperity. Frequently voted one of the most attractive streets in the country, the architecture of John Dobson Street reflects the city's former aspirations and status as an industrial powerhouse of engineering, shipbuilding, and export, most famously coal.

In thinking about Newcastle, coal remains the story people are most familiar with. The closures of pits, shipyards and their aftermath has often been depicted in popular culture. Sometimes sympathetically, and sometimes accompanied by 1980s comedy and caricature, such as Harry Enfield's Geordie 'Bugger All Money' character, Andy Capp comic strips, and the adult comic magazine *Viz*. There's no denying the devastating impact the loss of industry had on the region, or the long-term effects of unemployment, yet we must be cautious our history doesn't prevent us from seeing the city around us now.

# INTRODUCTION

If Newcastle itself could tell only one story it would be one of adaptation. It has responded to the challenges of deindustrialisation and decades of government under-investment by aspiring to become a centre of learning, the arts, and tourism. Looking around the quayside alone, it appears to be thriving. The landscape is vastly different from how it was in previous decades. The sites of former industry have been redeveloped into prestigious hotels, restaurants and luxury apartments. The area has never looked so good. Yet looks can be deceptive. Within an economy largely dependent on retail and the leisure industry, underemployment has become a problem. Poverty is no longer the simplistic black and white picture politicians once painted, a condition exclusive to the unemployed, the 'skivers', not 'strivers'. Under austerity, the demand for food banks across the region has soared by 20 per cent within the last year alone[1] – with zero-hour contracts and benefit delays being cited as the source. Ken Loach's film *I, Daniel Blake* (2016), with its scenes of benefit sanctions, poverty and hunger, is far from fiction for many; it is, sadly, a reality.

This isn't to say the city lacks hope. The response of volunteers within the region highlights a strong sense of community, recently demonstrated in the increased provision of food for families over the summer holidays in areas including Byker, the West End, and Benwell. Newcastle is stronger than the blows it has been dealt. This is what we wanted to reflect in *The Book of Newcastle*.

The project didn't happen overnight. Like the city itself, it evolved. It began as a call out by Comma Press in 2004 for a chapbook called *Newcastle Stories* to be distributed with *The Crack*. The book has come some 15 years later. Much has changed both globally and nationally since the first publication. The financial crash has affected both the region and the stories we received. Many of the original submissions

## INTRODUCTION

were more aspirational, focused on the social ladder and the dream of a quayside apartment. More than a decade later, in the wake of austerity, such subjects feel like fairy tales. The stories we received this second time around felt grittier. It seemed not only that people's prospects had changed, but that the short story itself had changed, too.

It is difficult to imagine now, with recent projects born both in and outside of the area (including Kit De Waal's *Common People* anthology, And Other Stories' Northern Book Prize, Dead Ink's *Test Signal* Kickstarter and the Northern Fiction Alliance) striving to acknowledge working-class writers and northern voices, but the idea of writing stories about the north still seemed unusual when this project initially began as *Newcastle Stories*. Within the context of an industry largely based in London, many writers felt discouraged from writing about where they were from. To write about the north was often to be marginalised, with some agents and publishers advising their clients to lose any accents in their work and write more upwardly mobile characters. Though it was seldom spoken out loud, to write about Newcastle was usually to write about being working class. There weren't many people encouraging that. It feels like such attitudes are slowly changing. There has never been a better time to write about where we come from. Not only socially or geographically, but in terms of how those places shape us, and who we are because of them.

In inviting the authors featured in this collection to write stories based on Newcastle upon Tyne, neither I nor my co-editor, Zoe Turner, suggested what anyone should write about. As editors, we didn't feel that was our job. Our mission was to create a space where writers could think about Newcastle, and the lives that the city shapes. Jessica Andrews' story is a wonderfully visceral response to that brief; in 'Blood Brothers', Newcastle forms the life-force

# INTRODUCTION

that runs between two girls – it's in their blood.

The stories we have commissioned here vary, yet all of them engage with key aspects of the city as integral to our lives; its landmarks, development, housing and parks. Many stories feature the 'Tyneside flat', a Victorian solution to providing decent, affordable housing in densely populated areas which remains a key aspect of living in the city. Of the seven different places I've rented in Newcastle and Gateshead, all have been Tyneside flats. Popular with students, young families, and older people alike, this type of accommodation is perhaps the opposite of student apartment block living. It is to live alongside people of varying ages and cultures. In 'Thunder Thursday on Pemberton Grove', J. A. Mensah utilises this phenomenon almost as a character itself; a structure that both separates and locks people together, allowing their lives to overlap.

There's more to Newcastle than limited personal space, of course. The Tyneside flat model goes hand in hand with the need for parks. During its boom, the strength of the city's planning policy lay in its acknowledgement of this. In addition to the new infrastructure, the 18th century brought residents the town moor, a common land of 1000 acres, Leaze's Park – in response to a worker's petition for leisure grounds – and Jesmond Dene. Just a mile or so from the city centre, Lord Armstrong gifted the Dene to the public upon his death for everyone to enjoy its wealth of birdsong, waterfalls, and trees. If we were to draw only from the imagery of popular culture, people may be forgiven for imagining Newcastle as a grey space of flat caps and cobbled lanes, yet the city remains a surprisingly green place.

The stories in this collection that feature such space remind us of its importance. Crista Ermiya's story, 'Duck Race', is rooted within the terraces of Heaton, yet opens into the Dene and the Ouseburn. There's a sense of liberation for Elle in leaving the flat full of her possessions; she seems less oppressed by her status, and is able to find light relief in the sights of a summer's day. Degna Stone also addresses this in 'Ekow on Town Moor'. It doesn't feel like this story of a man on the run could happen on a treadmill in Eldon Square Leisure. The moor rushes headlong at the protagonist, dragging his whole life along with it.

In stark contrast, the stories of the quayside acknowledge development and the increasing importance of the arts. Though literature may not be most people's first thought when considering Newcastle, the city has a proud literary history. In the 18$^{th}$ century, Newcastle was the country's fourth-biggest centre of printing, a contributing factor to establishing The Literary and Philosophical Library, which remains the largest independent library outside of London today. Sean O'Brien's story, 'Tabs', is a love song to libraries and the relationships that are formed within. It doesn't seem his characters would know each other without them. We are left wondering, what happens to the people who need libraries? When things change, where do they go? These are now crucial questions, considering the threat placed upon libraries by austerity. In 2013, Newcastle Council announced plans to close seventeen of its libraries (80 per cent), with others, including those in Jesmond and High Heaton, managing to survive only by depending on volunteers, and drastically reducing their opening hours.

The consequence of such constant flux is that, living in Newcastle, it is never quite possible to be in 'the here and now' without the lingering presence of the past. Margaret Wilkinson's story about the neglected Westgate Hill Cemetery speaks of this space where the past and the future converge. This awareness of the past is perhaps unavoidable for the residents of Newcastle. The development of former industrial

## INTRODUCTION

sites, such as Ouseburn Valley into a centre for the arts and creative industries, indicates what the future may hold if we can hold onto progress. But, with cuts to the arts under austerity, including to organisations like Seven Stories – the national centre for children's books housed within a renovated Victorian mill – the city is reminded of how difficult holding onto such progress can be. Though Newcastle wants to move beyond the shadow of the past, under-investment leaves the future uncertain. The current increase in poverty is a painful reminder of a difficult part of our history and the jobs lost under Thatcherism. Famously, Thatcher labelled the 1 in 5 people who were unemployed in the North East as 'moaning minnies', again belittling the region's working class. The damage caused by such slurs and stereotyping doesn't disappear overnight. The wounds such comments leave in our sense of regional pride have taken decades to heal.

Such an awareness of Newcastle's past within its present was with us throughout the process of editing this collection, when we chose to include writers who are, sadly, no longer with us. Julia Darling and Chrissie Glazebrook's work felt like an important part of Newcastle's literary legacy, and we wanted to continue to celebrate it alongside the city's contemporary writers. At a time when much of the industry seemed reluctant to embrace stories about Newcastle or the north more generally, their writing gave others permission to use their regional voices and acknowledge the city. Perhaps even more importantly, their work still feels as fresh as it did when it was first read. The story 'Living on Planet Clacky', by another of our original contributors, Glynis Reed, has a quality that doesn't age. It sweeps us along breathlessly with its unapologetically northern voice, where the details of working-class life become animated by an understated humour. Here we are, this is us, in this glorious city, it says, get in! There is no more we can ask of any story, but for it to

## INTRODUCTION

take us on a journey to a whole other place. We hope you enjoy your stay in Newcastle.

*Angela Readman*
*Newcastle, October 2019*

## Note

1. https://www.chroniclelive.co.uk/news/north-east-news/food-banks-prepare-desperate-summer-16593160

# Calling From Newcastle

## Julia Darling

'WHAT CAN YOU SEE?' asked the person at the other end of the line. 'I mean, really. Where are you?'

Gloria hung up. You weren't supposed to hang up.

When Gloria went for the job at the call centre, she was shy. She tried to make herself shrink. She wore a loose black top, a dark brown skirt and flat shoes.

The call centre was a square box between roundabouts on the edge of a ring road just outside Newcastle. It was clever, she thought, the way it seemed to have no windows when in fact from the inside you could see out. If Gloria stood up, she could see some bullocks in a narrow field. She liked the way they changed position, arranging themselves like compositions for her benefit, sometimes running up and down the field shaking their young, wild heads. It was unusual to have a view in this kind of work. Most people sat in cubicles, boxed in by thin screens.

The job interview had been hurried and officious. So many people didn't stay, the interviewer said. What were her plans?

'I've left school,' she said, 'my family is here. I've got no plans to go anywhere.'

The truth was she didn't know. She had passed exams. She could go to university if she wanted, but she couldn't imagine sleeping in a narrow bed in a strange town. Her parents told her to take things slowly, to take a year to think about what she wanted, to dream a little. Friends from school were going to Mexico, to dig ditches in China, build schools in Malawi, but Gloria had never been on an aeroplane, and she was unlikely to go to somewhere where they spoke a foreign language when she found the idea of York or Warwick alarming. And she loved her family. She liked the way they sat still, understanding one another, always thinking the best of each other. Most families were at each other's throats.

She had been for other jobs. She'd answered an advert for a receptionist in Mal Maison, a swanky hotel on the edge of the River Tyne, just by the sleek bone of the new bridge. They asked her for an interview. She had worn a red velour top that was old for her age, but which her mother had thought looked sophisticated. The interview only lasted five minutes. Gloria sat on a velvet chaise-longue in a Bakelite room with a crisp, ice faced young woman behind a desk who had taken down her details with a silver fountain pen, then said they would be in touch.

She had tried shop work too, working in Next, but they had turned her away.

She knew why. She was eighteen stone. She moved slowly, breathing heavily. She was a giantess. On the other hand, her voice was light as blancmange and clear. It was the voice of a bright eighteen-year-old woman.

The call centre lapped her up. In the grey building, no one knew what size you were. After the interview eight of them were invited for training. She found herself with seven others, all shy, all sweet-voiced. Some had acne, some were very tall, others had twitches. It was a meeting of all the people who had never been picked for teams in sports classes.

They sat in a circle with their arms folded across their chests and were shown how to sell insurance, how to raise a fist in the air if there was a bomb scare, how to behave when customers were rude. Mark, the supervisor, was a young man who rarely smiled. He wore a tight white shirt and the skin on his neck was over-washed and red. Gloria wondered if he might have a cleanliness phobia when she saw him wiping his biro with a handkerchief.

For six pounds an hour Gloria sat in a cubicle selling house insurance, over and over again, next to a young man called Gareth with large teeth, who smiled at her sometimes, and who once gave her a mint. One day they stood together watching the bullocks gathering into a tight group around a pile of new hay.

'I like animals,' Gareth had said.

'Me too,' answered Gloria.

Then they had shrugged helplessly, knowing there was nothing more to be said, and returned to their cramped cubicles.

'Where are you?' asked the woman at the end of the line.

'It's just a job,' Gloria replied. 'I'm in a building in the North.'

The woman was from central London. They were usually the unfriendly ones, but she kept on asking questions.

'How do I know you're not in Budapest?' she asked Gloria. 'You could be anywhere.'

'I suppose I could,' said Gloria, 'but I'm in Newcastle.'

Gloria had always been big. Her mother was monumental, and her father was generous and bearded. She had three brothers, and all of them were sturdy, well built, with polished cheeks and wide arms and legs. At family occasions, rooms weren't big enough for all of them, and they often hired hotels at Christmas and for birthdays.

Sometimes Gloria's father came to pick her up after work. He liked to tell Gloria about the coal mine that had been on the site of the call centre. His father had been a miner. He said that once the whole place had been cluttered with blackened men and noise, and now it was as if someone had pushed it all underground and covered it up with grass and roundabouts and well-behaved cows.

Gloria was good at selling house insurance. Her voice was honest and she was always very polite. If there was a baby crying, or a dog barking she always sympathised and said she would phone back later.

It was hard to remember the actual point when Gloria began to lie. It wasn't because she was unhappy, or restless. Afterwards, she thought that it was to do with the bullocks. One day, as she stood up to go to the toilet, she glanced through the narrow window and saw that the field was empty. At first, she thought they had been moved temporarily, but then they didn't return. It was as if a part of Gloria sagged a little.

Then Gareth, from the next cubicle, with eczema and thin shoulders, hung himself. Gloria read about him in the local paper. She felt angry. No one had said anything at the call centre. The next day, in the staff room, she told Marsha and Ann as they sat eating pot noodles. They looked back at her with sad, watery eyes.

'Why?' asked Ann.

'No one knows.'

'You could get depressed, working here. No one would care,' said Gloria, softly.

'Yes,' said Marsha.

'We could get some flowers,' said Ann. 'We should do something.'

So they had clubbed together and bought some lilies, and put them on Gareth's chair. Mark looked confused, but didn't move them, and it was only when a new person started a week later that the dead flowers were thrown away.

Gloria phoned a number in Bristol. A man answered. He sounded as if he had just woken up and was lying in bed.

'You've got a nice voice,' he said.

'Thank you,' said Gloria.

'Where are you?' he asked.

'I'm in the desert,' said Gloria. 'In a modern building. From where I am sitting, I can see a long line of camels.'

'Are you serious?' asked the man. Gloria imagined him rubbing his forehead, smiling, glancing up at the grey sky through the window.

'Absolutely,' said Gloria. 'You should see the light. It's golden. Everything is filled with warm light.'

'I wish I was there,' said the man.

'Are you interested in budget insurance?' asked Gloria.

'Not really. But the desert sounds good.'

Gloria put the phone down. She felt as if someone was standing behind her, but when she turned there was no one there.

The staff room was brown, and pockmarked, with long grey sofas. At one end you could smoke, but the whole room smelt of tobacco. Gloria sat with Deborah, whose body was like a pile of sandbags and who had hard red eyes. Gloria told her what she'd said and Deborah snorted.

'If only,' she said.

'Are you happy working here?' asked Gloria.

Deborah shrugged. 'It's a job,' she said.

'I'm in Iceland,' said Gloria. 'It never gets dark. There are whales out there. I was brought up by Eskimos, but I speak perfect English.'

'Is that right?' asked a man with a voice like a deep furrow.

'Where are you?' asked Gloria.

'In Sunderland,' said the man. 'I was a welder, but now I'm a security guard.'

'I know the North East,' said Gloria. 'I had a friend there, called Gareth, but unfortunately, he hung himself.'

'I'm sorry about that,' whispered the man.

'He worked in a call centre,' continued Gloria. 'He never went out.'

'A lot of people jump off bridges in the North East,' said the man. 'It's not all as rosy as they make out, the new millennium. I thought about it once myself.'

'Do you want to buy insurance?' asked Gloria, aware that Mark hovered behind her.

'Maybe,' said the man. Mark moved on, rubbing his neck with a tissue.

'Tell me about Sunderland, then,' said Gloria, 'sometimes I get tired of snow.'

'I grew up here. I can't see it from outside,' said the man. 'It's canny, but that's because my family are here.'

'I know what you mean,' said Gloria. 'I don't think Gareth had family. That was part of the problem.'

The man agreed to receive information through the post. That week Gloria was top employee.

But Gloria couldn't stop dreaming. On her day off she went into town, wearing a bright red scarf and matching hat, moving slowly through the Saturday crowds at Monument, the animal liberationist stalls, the discordant chimes of a busker playing the xylophone. She bought an atlas and a book about world travel. She started to memorise facts about different countries.

That weekend she also became a vegetarian. She couldn't stop thinking about the bullocks that had disappeared. She was afraid, in some coincidental way, that she might end up eating a part of one of them in a pie, and she found that idea horrifying, so horrifying that it made her retch.

'I mean, where do you people come from?' asked a woman with a voice like ripping silk.

'I'm calling from the Falklands,' said Gloria. 'They've recruited a thousand telephonists from the UK and sent us all out here. We live in dormitories. It's horrible. The sky is grey, and there are remains of war everywhere, like old shells and shipwrecks.'

'Are you serious?'

'Absolutely. I should never have left the North East. That's where I belong.'

'My husband was a soldier,' said the woman, 'but…' then her voice broke up, and Gloria could hear her sliding away from the telephone, replacing the handset.

'I think we should go out,' said Gloria, to Marsha, Deborah and Ann. 'We should go out together and talk.'

The three young women looked at her suspiciously. They were all afraid of the outside world.

'Come on!' said Gloria. 'Why not?'

She wasn't sure where her confidence was coming from. It was as if she had found a tap somewhere inside herself and turned it on, and her dried-up soul was growing green shoots.

So they met, under the statue of a golden lady above a jewellers in the centre of town. They walked together down the Bigg Market arm in arm, taking up all the pavement. The ground trembled underneath their weight. Men, giddy at the sight of them, stood back and applauded. One man shouted 'The heifers are out!'

They squeezed through forests of thin, sapling bodies in clubs, right to the centre of the dance floor, then shimmied and kicked, arm in arm. They got mortal on Bloody Mary's, vodka and ice, Tia-Maria. Deborah was sick in her handbag. Marsha lost the heel of her shoe. They ended up having to get two taxis home as they couldn't fit into one.

They promised to go out together every Thursday.

'Not another one,' moaned a voice at the end of the phone. 'I am sick of this. I bet you're sitting somewhere in India, aren't you? I hate what's happening to the world. I don't want insurance. I don't want anything. Where are you? Eh?'

'In Newcastle,' said Gloria. 'This is where I live.'

'You sound like a nice person. What are you doing a job like that for?'

'Because no one else would have me,' said Gloria.

'It makes me sad,' moaned the voice, 'no one speaks to anyone else anymore.'

'You have to try harder that's all,' said Gloria. 'Go on. What are you doing sitting inside at this time of day?'

'I'm in a wheelchair,' said the voice.

'So what,' said Gloria. 'I'm eighteen stone.'

Then she hung up, raised her fist in the air and shouted 'BOMB SCARE!' just for the hell of it, and everyone had to leave the building, stampeding down the concrete steps like a herd of freed beasts, out into the green and blue of daylight.

# Magpies

## Angela Readman

THERE'S ANOTHER ONE AT the window scraping its beak on the glass. I stare at the magpie. It stares back, cocks its head to one side. It appears fascinated by its reflection. The glaze of its feathers. The pricks of its eyes.

*Good morning, Captain, I salute you. One for sorrow. Two for joy.* All that jazz. I don't greet magpies the way other people do though. I pour Cheerio's in my palm and say, 'Hey, you…' The bird observes me. Hair lank from the shower, bath towel knotted around my chest. I inch closer, reach for the lock. It flies off, less afraid than bored with me.

The pecked pane is frosty, criss-crossed; a hashtag *#magpieswerehere*. I stroke the glass like a scab. Outside, the street flutters. Rubbish sacks picked to black ribbons; soup cans roll in the wind.

The litter's a problem. The council sent leaflets warning us not to make it worse. *Dispose of litter responsibly. Do not feed the birds.* The diagram resembled a *NO SMOKING* sign, a red line crossed through a corvid's silhouette as if it would kill us. The woman across the street couldn't care less.

She opens her window and tosses toast into the yard. The slice slides along the lean-to of the flat downstairs, Nutella and butter slipping down the plastic like a streaked clock. It's still there after an hour. We watch it, the woman and I, another Sunday gliding by.

★

It was a different sort of Sunday when Tone lost it. Roast chicken in the oven, and a paperback on the sofa from my holy hour alone. The boys made their own churches, pulling their shirts over their heads in the drizzle. They kicked a ball around the park. It was June, and all summer pattered and scolded. A slack winter had allowed the wild bird population to spiral out of control. The magpies were the worst. They were everywhere, streaking the city, stealing the chicks of smaller birds. It was difficult to sleep for their rasp, like laughter, Tone said. Whenever one started, another joined in. He got so sick of it he bought an air rifle.

I stopped him firing, clamping my hand across the gun. He left the following day between shifts. Packed his wok, his radio and Siracha. On his way out, I said, 'Don't forget your gun.'

I didn't tell Zack until after work. 'Whatever,' he said, 'I didn't like him anyway.'

He plugged in his skull-buds and took down the football posters in his room, claiming he couldn't be arsed. Thought their kick arounds were stupid anyway, it wasn't like he was going to be a pro or anything. 'I only went cos he seemed desperate to be friends. I felt sorry for him,' he said, shoving the football shirt from his wall into a sack.

The space where it hung left a bright torso above the bed, the wallpaper a stranger to daylight. I bought another poster to pin in its place. Collective nouns. They'd obsessed us last year after seeing a wildlife documentary: *A clown of Puffins, a leash of deer, a sleuth of bears.*

Zack's favourite was a *skulk of foxes*. Painting the kitchen, every so often, we'd call out nouns to one another like inventors. *A blaze of foxes, a cardinal, a glint.* No, skulk was killer.

I stretched out the poster to show him, but Zack didn't take it.

'I'm kind of over that,' he said, 'it's sort of pathetic.'

I rolled up the poster to put in my own room after we moved. *A nostalgia of mothers, a folly, a pang of sons.*

★

It was windier on this side of the bridge, Newcastle spilling across the river like a glass puzzle scattered in the water. Gateshead perching above it, breaking the back of the wind. Zack joked that all the sunshine got steered to the city, to pretty up the view from The Hilton. He hated us moving to Gateshead, but after Tone left it all came down to rent. I let him sulk through the weekends, eyes glued to his phone. The kids he'd known were now a bus and a metro away, the ones at school still just a blur of faces in a corridor.

'I have popcorn, a slasher and nachos,' I said.

'You're on.'

We tossed a blanket over the rain and curled up with a movie, a bowl of popcorn between us on the couch for experimental flavour Saturday. Salt and chilli flakes. Bacon bits and brown sugar. When texts from his Heaton Manor friends began to dwindle, we gorged on teenagers racing through the woods. Mean ones and stoned ones. The ones who smoked and had sex, meeting a sticky end while the smart girl survived. It lasted until August, when I came in with more nachos and found him lacing his trainers.

'You off out?'

He grabbed his jacket, an arm branching across me. I winced. I'd nursed him by the window as a baby, not caring who saw. I'd wanted only to hold him to the light, see the sun pick the colours out of his fair hair like a loose string of sequins. I was sorry it had darkened, sorry to see his face suddenly so oily.

'You meeting Benji? I can spring for bus fare.'

'Nah, it's alright.'

He'd found new friends that didn't have names like Benji, a kid with a Buddha belly who once laughed until he peed watching *Paddington*. These friends were cooler, older, and used only their surnames like soldiers. He mentioned so many I couldn't keep up.

'I want you in by ten,' I called. He came in at eleven, claiming his phone died. I rang it and saw the lie light up his pocket.

'I just wanted to stay out longer,' he said, scratching his shoulder. 'I don't see the point in curfews anyway. If I was gonna get killed or summat, I'd die just as much at ten as eleven.' He pulled his sleeves over his hands, let them dangle. 'It's a joke! God, the look on your face.'

I had no idea what my face looked like. His laugh still reminded me of a kid who didn't really get what was funny but giggled anyway.

\*

I let him sleep late on payday and walked into Gateshead. The supermarket always made me think about dying. Whenever I saw it, I pictured the car park that used to be on the same spot, where Michael Caine had pushed a gangster over the barrier in *Get Carter*. The falling man looked graceful for a second before landing. That always surprised me. I could remember nothing else about the film.

The security guard blinked in the foyer confronting a difficult customer.

'I'm sorry, you can't put flyers up here,' he said. 'Against store policy.'

The woman stuck a poster to the window. I knew her. Not her name, but the sight of her. A woman who lived in the street behind us and seemed to wear nothing but tracksuits. This one was fuchsia. The velour frosted and bloomed as she moved, stepping closer to the guard.

'See this,' she said holding up a photo that looked like a Boxing Day snap. A fifteen-year-old lad; fuzzied by a Tigger onesie, uncool for a day to please his mam. 'He hasn't come home for days,' she said. 'What if it was your kid?'

The guard wiped his glasses. Shoppers rattled past; trolleys nosed onto the travellator. He directed her to the car park where she could do what she liked. 'If anyone asks,' he said, 'I saw nothing.'

I carried my groceries up Bensham Bank. The sky peeling silver, flecked with cloud. A flock of magpies congregated outside the carwash, picking at a rag on the forecourt. *A crook, a bruise, a radge of magpies.* The lads valeting BMWs looked wary, outnumbered. The birds were brazen. They'd been known to hop into shops and hop out with a beak full of stolen crisps and Snickers. Some businesses had even started to lay poison, though it wasn't advised. It was impossible to know just where any bird's heart may stop. Not all would flit off and die quietly. Some spiralled from the air mid-flight, striking anything in their path.

The wind lifted and loosened the posters on the lampposts. Underneath the kid in the onesie was an older poster of some kid in a cap, his faded face wrinkled by rain. *Missing, Missing.* The paper fluttered all along the hill, lorries charging past.

★

He went out on Friday night and I cleaned the flat, a movie keeping me company. Some girl running from a killer in a mask. I reached Zack's room last. His bedroom door had looked grubby by the time we left the old place, dulled by years of my inching it open just a crack, to check on him on my way to bed, the soft waft of his sleepy breathing, sweet as muffins. The gloss here was fresh.

The air smelt musky. Pungent beyond the usual scent of socks, damp towels and boy. I looked around, picked up a furry mug by the bed and lifted the valance. There were stale sandwich crusts underneath, a rotten apple and sweet wrappers. I reached under, found a few spoons and pulled out a knife.

It didn't look dangerous. It looked ordinary. Practical. Not designed for hunting or anything, but cutting vegetables, meat. I sat in the lounge and held the knife like a horizon. The silky green handle, the blade. I'd never seen it before.

Zack came in when the movie was finished and the girl was safe, for now.

'You been in my room?' he said. He scratched his nose, blackheads peppering his freckles. 'It's not what you think. I got it for you. For like, your birthday,' he said. He scratched again.

'You're bleeding,' I said.

He rubbed his face, a blemish disturbed. I reached for a tissue and left it, recalling being fourteen. My mother lunging at a blackhead and showing me the tissue after. It looked like my shame wriggling out of me.

It was my birthday in a month. The cutlery in the drawer barely cut butter.

'We'll talk in the morning.' I handed him his pyjamas from the radiator. He stuffed them under his shirt, clutching the warmth to his chest on his way to bed. Just the same as I always did.

The letter arrived on Saturday before he was awake. I folded it into my pocket on my way to work, a flat space beneath my name badge. Zack had skipped school more than once.

I stood on the landing with my arms folded, my boots furry and pawlike beside his trainers.

'You're not going anywhere,' I said.

Zack took a step towards the door. The phone in his pocket vibrated. He glanced at it. Torn. I waited, blocking the stairs, aware of how easily he could push me out of his way. For a second, he looked like he was considering it, but couldn't. Not that sort of son yet.

'Whatever.' He rubbed his head and went to his room. I let out a breath, a small feather drifting in the air, slight as a pillow fight.

★

He wouldn't speak to me in the morning. I heard his phone, then I heard nothing. I popped my head around his bedroom door expecting to find him gone, footprints on the drainpipe like something from a film, but he was still there.

'You want anything from the shop? I was going to make a full English. You fancy it?'

He loved his eggs scrambled with coriander. Bacon so crunchy it cracked like a rib.

'Nope,' he said.

'How about a movie later?'

'Nope.'

He scratched his knuckles beneath his hoodie. Always so sensitive, his hands, prone to flare-ups and flakes. Baby eczema, dermatitis. In primary school, they got so sore in winter that he couldn't use soap to wash them before lunch. He struggled with cutlery; fingers slippery with emollient. They looked even worse now. The skin was so cracked I thought of a game from my childhood. Holding out one hand for another girl to scratch, a fingernail scraping a tendon. Idling over the same patch of skin, again and again, long enough for it to weep. The winner was whoever had to stop first. The girl scratching, or the one who bled.

'Did you do that scratching?' I asked, 'Or was it something else?

I reached for Zack's hand. He pulled away, his eyes dark, pupils dilated.

'Just leave us alone, will yer.'

I closed the door behind me. Let him sulk. He'll come around. Just give him space.

*

The flowers glistened outside the grocers, a shrine of plastic and rain. Three girls huddled outside the launderette at half term, palms cupped to the hot breath of the air vents. I heard them singing as I passed. Harmonising. Not loud enough for the whole street to hear, just loud enough to hear themselves. 'There Is a Light That Never Goes Out,' like a requiem.

No one had found a body, only clothes outside the church; the ones the boy in the Tigger onesie had been wearing when he was last seen. Tattered. Bits of hoodie, leggings, and sad scraps of cotton that were once underwear. The cloth was flecked with blood. Tiny spots of it. His. The girls lay chrysanthemums in the spot where the clothes had been found. The pavement looked horribly clean. It reminded me of an accident the year Zack was born, outside The Tyneside. Seeing the concrete afterwards, it had looked so much paler than the rest of the city. Greaseless, pressure-washed, spotless.

'I hate this.' The boy's mother walked out of the launderette and snatched up the flowers from the path. Blonde hair funnelling around her face, her velour tracksuit dove grey. 'He's still alive,' she said, 'I'm sure of it.'

She looked at me when she spoke, her eyes small and watery. I nodded, hugging my bacon, unsure what to say. I wondered if I'd seen her so many times without smiling, it was too late to start.

*

I listened for the bathroom when Zack didn't leave his room. Running water, a flush, any sign that he was awake. I figured he was pissing in bottles just to avoid me. It was his job to take out the rubbish, but I did it myself. Magpies clattering on the bins behind me, their skittery claws on the plastic. I finally cooked up a peace offering at ten. Fresh chips with cheese. I carried them to his room with a can of Coke under my arm.

'Just leave it, I'll have it later,' he said.

He didn't reach for the plate, though I saw he'd cleared it by the morning. It looked like he'd been ravenous during the night. I found the kitchen littered with crumbs, a mosaic of crushed crackers on the floor. I rubbed pickle off the counter and discovered the fridge was empty. The bacon was gone, though there was no pan or crockery in the sink.

I knocked and went in. Zack lay on his bed in a vest, foetal, arms wrapped around himself and scratching his shoulders. It surprised me how little of him there was without his hoodie and coat. The arcs of his shoulder blades jutted like the millennial bridge; I could count the vertebrae of his spine.

'Baby? You OK?' I lay a hand on his forehead and withdrew it, a stab of pain in my palm. The blackheads protruded, stubbly and sharp as pins. He shivered and scratched his bare arms. I hadn't expected to see blackheads there, too.

'Prickly,' he said, 'prickly all over.' He curled, rubbing his elbow, flakes of skin leaving silvery dust on the duvet. His knees jerked and a cramp folded him double.

I rushed to my phone in the kitchen, the doctor's number on there somewhere. I waited on hold. Vivaldi's 'Four Seasons' piped into my ear. The world wintering and budding on a loop.

'Ma...'

The cry pulled me through the flat. It rose long and high, falling as I reached the bedroom door. I nudged it open and a magpie flitted past me, brushing my cheek. The air flickered with birds, a flock of a dozen or more. Frantic wings bashed the walls. One then another flew into the window with a crack, leaving red smudges on the glass.

I saw no sign of Zack other than his clothes. Batman bottoms riddled with holes and his vest in shreds, a black and white feather caught in the cotton.

\*

I still have the feather. I keep it in my pocket, feel it between my fingers. The day and the night of it. I walk to Saltwell Park stroking it as the snow falls, dusting the dark railings, settling on the gate like a Tim Burton film. It's Baltic; the ice on the pond looks like a sack of dropped knives. I picture the Nutella freezing to the roof outside the flat. My duvet on the sofa, the fire and slouch socks. It's strange, but the place seems warmer when I'm not there. I can see it so vividly. I see a flock of magpies waiting in the lounge, just tame enough to peck crumbs from my palm. If I hold out my hand long enough, a head may butt my fingertip. Jostle for a stroke.

I imagine that I didn't go to the window that day. I picture myself not ducking through the flock and flinging it open, the smack of wings against the glass too awful to bear. I didn't think about it, that reflex. If you find a bird in the house, you let it out.

I watched the flock leave. *The charm, the tiding, the murder,* as many nouns for magpies as moods of a son. They flickered over the flats like a kid's drawing of home, capped by sunshine and bluebirds. Only one didn't leave immediately, but paused. It sat on the sill looking at me for a while. I reached out a finger and it was off. I still put food out for it sometimes.

I see others do the same. The woman across the lane, casting out bread. These women in the park dropping cornflakes in the powdery snow, sprinkling crisps under benches. I nod as we pass, recognise them as my tribe. *A sorrow of mothers, a worry, a clutch, a nurture, a brood.* Our eyes meet and our lips move, before we look up, away.

# Tabs

## Sean O'Brien

THE PRINTED NOTICE ON the big table at the far end of the library was so discreet you might have thought it referred to something mundane, like the Easter closing hours – the kind of information the members acquired by osmosis anyway. In fact, it stated that from 31 March – 'in line with trends elsewhere in society in general' - smoking would be banned in the library.

*Change and decay in all around I see.* Surely, though, the library wasn't subject to the same processes and historical forces as 'elsewhere'. It was the *library*: an ancient institution where you had to pay a subscription to join, supposing the committee's inquisitors judged you fit for membership. If all went well and you got past the caretaker and up the stone stairs you were safe in 1964, or 1958, or, if you preferred, 1913, when all the world smoked. The authority of 'elsewhere' was suspended: that was the point. *Smoking*, and smoking-affiliated activities like sitting around, like waiting, like passing the time between one thing finished and the next beginning – these, not reading and writing, gave the library its *raison d'être*. It was a smoking library – damn few others like it anywhere. And now the lights were going out all over Europe.

There had been a time when the smoking ban would have meant a row. There would have been resignations and calls for extraordinary meetings. And, though it would have made no difference to the outcome, there would have been impassioned mutterings around the big table. It was the headquarters of a *salon des refusés* of the law and the academy. This shifting group of desperate men clung to the idea of house-ownership and the life of the mind by their fingertips there at the smoky hub of the library, like Balzacian gamblers leaving the wheel of their ruined fortunes only to drink and to pawn their last possessions. The fraternity of the big table passed the days by looking at the nudes in *Practical Photography,* rolling cigarettes and writing endless letters of application to ever more obscure law firms and institutions of higher education. Their low chorus of dissent could be heard as a reassuring background, however far away you sat. Even in the remote monastic setting of the Silence Room in the sub-basement among the county archives they could be heard, like a warning in a foreign language. Now, I realised, they too were gone, somehow – never noticed them go – and in a week or two smoking would be gone as well. The library was much too quiet.

What would remain, at least for a time, were the oily encrustations which had grown slowly, like black reefs of disease, over the books shelved in the upper galleries. You could find all sorts up there where the poets went to die – early Auden, MacNeice, Empson, alongside historical curiosities with local connections like Michael Roberts (Longbenton) and Francis Scarfe (South Shields). There was even, mysteriously, an original 1923 edition of Wallace Stevens's *Harmonium*: upstairs, it sweated tar like Eliot's Thames. By and large the diseased yellow air of these autumnal upper galleries was the haunt of librarians. They shifted the smoke-diseased stock from shelf to shelf, like nineteenth-century doctors sending their doomed consumptive patients from spa to spa. Among the sufferers were Mann's *The Magic Mountain* and Katherine Mansfield's stories – sick books that no one read now or cared to be reminded of, shunted off to heaven's gate and replaced by crime novels and lite lit for lowbrow ladies. It is of course unfair to associate the decline of smoking with the death of the educated general reader: after all, one is a fact and the other merely a suspicion, and all they have in common is simultaneity. But still. Anyway, the chances were you could get hold of the Wallace Stevens if you cared to ascend the wrought-iron spiral staircase into the previous century. Then, one day, *Harmonium* wasn't there.

It was down on the big table, it turned out, lying unopened next to a packet of tobacco, some liquorice Rizlas and a lighter the shape of a U-boat conning tower. The saturnine Harry Box was looking at the book as he rolled a cigarette. He continued to look at the book as he lit the cigarette. He renewed his scrutiny as he exhaled the first drag.

'Are you using that?' I asked.

'Ahuh.'

'I mean the copy of *Harmonium*.'

'Ahuh.'

I picked up the *TLS* and waited. A couple of years later, he glanced up and said: *'Fill your black hull / With white moonlight. // There will never be an end / To this droning of the surf.'* He seemed to expect a reply.

'Stevens.'

'Course it is.'

'From *Harmonium*.'

'Course it is.'

There seemed to be no way forward from here. Harry looked a shade disappointed.

'Tell you what.'

'Yes?'

'It's fuckin' mint, mind. Whatever any cunt says.'

To the best of my knowledge, no cunt had disparaged Stevens lately. It took me a moment to recognise, in the present context, an example of the pre-emptive aggression, directed at imagined slights, which characterises this fascinating part of the country. Honour satisfied, Harry rose and put his papers into his carrier bag, along with the copy of *Harmonium*, then left the building. He did not stop to check the book out at the issue desk. *Harmonium* may have been the property of the library, but it was Harry Box who really owned it. When I had used the book before, it had merely been on loan from Harry. I was intrigued.

Harry Box, was sometimes physically in, but never professionally *of*, the Applicants Anonymous group at the big table. For one thing he had a job – some undefined lecturing post at a college south of the river – politics or history, I never knew exactly. Attired in his patented gloom, wearing the aromatic pall of his steady consumption, he continued to quote Stevens spontaneously from time to time over the next few years. These occasions were like Bank Holidays in a Trappist monastery. *Ramon Fernandez, tell me if you can… The world is ugly and the people are sad… Upon a hill in Tennessee.* He delivered a line, then seemed to listen to it fading in time, smiling through his smoke as if it pleased him that this was the case. Thus we approached the Millennium – the ageing youths and Harry and myself, riding the table like a raft while storms elsewhere consumed unlucky mariners by the shipload.

Like many men of a certain age, out in the badlands, a few years short of forty, Harry made a big performance of the hand-rolled cigarette. He made it into an *activity*. For the duration of the making, until he nipped off a couple of loose threads of *Old Hawser*, or whatever he was smoking that week, you believed him: this was the preface to something decisive; a deed was imminent, of which all this fadge was simply the herald. Rolling a cigarette was more than a way of occupying the meantime; it was substantial and meaningful behaviour. It spoke for a world, the one at which Harry gestured through the smoke as he breathed it out in rings: the world of Stevens and the library, the bridges and the river that ran darkly beneath them, of the river's mouth and the vast satisfactory distances beyond, from here to either pole and on to Singapore and Valparaiso. Even Harry's moustache was involved in the smoke somehow, and thus in that wider world where the atlas was mainly blue, where yawning depths were crossed by vessels with Harry's rolling tobacco secreted in their bilges, like contraband. God, the man could smoke.

One day he put an open book down on the table in front of me.

'Look at that.'

I read where his yellow finger pointed: *Take a last turn / In the tang of possibility.*'

'That's what I mean,' he said. 'Do you know what I mean?'

'I think so.'

'I wanted to be a ship's navigator. I took the vision test. Turned out I was colour blind.' He smiled through the smoke, closed the copy of Heaney's *Wintering Out* and went back to reading Stevens. You could feel the globe waiting, still patient, for someone to cross it, for Harry to give up his self-possession and simply *go*. Colour blindness was only a setback. There were other means of travel. *Tout est luxe, calme et volupte.* Surely there was time. I was anxious for Harry's sake that this should be the case: anxious, I mean, that the imagination should be vindicated in its travels. For around the same time, equally unexpectedly, he showed me a handful of poems.

Normally this is a signal to make one's excuses and leave, if necessary starting a new life in a different part of the country. Beware of trespassing in the realm of green ink and alternative spelling, where the obsessed are waiting to waylay you with their lives' work. But Harry's poems were interesting. They drew on the Baudelaire of 'Le Voyage', on Rimbaud and Conrad and RLS and other seagoing literature of all kinds – and of course on Stevens, who, like Harry, never went anywhere, certainly never Abroad. Harry had Stevens's feel for the exotic. He could find it in the dancers – 'exotics' with the glottal 't' – in the clubs on Shields Road on Sunday lunchtimes, where Stevens probably would not; but Harry also understood the power of names: Tehuantepec, Valparaiso, Far Cathay, planted like a path of islands, further and further into the ocean. (*Where mind and ocean meet.* I realised that where other people had conversation, Harry had quotation and reference.) The combination of longing and pre-emptive disappointment had something of Laforgue about it, but at bottom it was all his own. It was as if in any encounter he had always just cast off, back into the smoke-filled Sargasso of his seemingly unshakeable preoccupations, steered by the self-possession whose one command was *not yet; manana*. His mode of conversation was always, I see now, the farewell.

We fell into the habit – I'm not sure exactly how or when – of drinking together on Wednesdays when the library closed early. We crossed the river by the High Level Bridge to sit among the resonant desolation and imminent violence of the Coffin Bar. We re-crossed the water to perform what Harry called 'a sector crawl', along the quayside as the developers took aim at its dozen old blokes' bars, or wandered up behind the hospital and into the fringes of the West End, where wise men always went equipped but literary types were safe because ignored. Our conversation was simple, repetitive and – to me – intensely pleasurable. It took in Wallace Stevens, Baudelaire, Rimbaud, modernism and the sea. Harry, I recognise now, said very little. He would launch a sentence, a quotation, an allusion, down the slipway of the evening and watch as it drifted from view. The evenings dissolved like smoke in the contemplation of fragments and gnomic *aperçus*. It was with

Harry that I developed a taste for Scotch, a dark mild made from the scrapings of ashtrays and the urine of smokers. When we were getting drunk, Harry would say, 'Out there, out there,' gesturing at the bar-room door or the gantry or the dartboard, but meaning the ocean, the immense, the sublime, the all-consuming dimension where the mind could drink, drown and be re-born at eternal leisure. The riches of those absconders' hours! Sometimes a withered glass collector in a Cyrenians' suit would nod agreement at one of Harry's sudden announcements and suddenly tell us that he had been regimental bantamweight champion, that he had caught a spectacular disease in Port Said, that he had fathered a child on a black woman in Durban and always meant to go back. Harry would nod: here was proof of all he intended. He would roll the man a cigarette and then suddenly we would be out in the street, walking briskly despite being half-cut. When I asked why, Harry would say: 'He's that unhappy.'

Harry was engaged, it seemed, to a primary school teacher, Anne. She remained a misty, notional figure. She was never the direct subject of his discourse: she only emerged as sort of grammatical necessity, with consequences for other kinds of statement, referred to in terms of having to go home eventually from whichever pub we had gone to when the library closed. Relations between the sexes seemed almost unrevised hereabouts in those days: men were selfish and women complained. It took a long time for people to realise that they could manage these roles independently. When they finally did, almost overnight entire streets ceased to have a male population. A female quiet of afternoon television commenced, broken only by the weekend departures of children with overnight bags. You saw them climbing into cars whose drivers preferred not to approach the house.

But that is to anticipate. Anne was a distant, more or less benevolent idea. I imagined her as a grown-up Grace Darling, ready in her mackintosh on playground duty to do the right thing if called upon. Even though I scarcely met her, like Harry she seemed in some way already historical, a beckoning figure in the rainy doorway of the Bridge or the Crown Posada or the Barking Dog, there to extract her man, with weary good humour, from the smoke-filled room of his choice and — dare one say it — his real affections.

'She seems nice,' I said.

'Aye, canny.'

Of course, we know nothing of other people's relationships, not really: so we tell ourselves. So I told myself that Harry's taciturn Geordismo was simply that, not an evasion of me (why need he bother? We were simply drinking companions), still less of his own life and of Anne. The mood I glimpsed between them was never of entrapped sadness on his part or of equally entrapped hopefulness on hers. Ignore that clock: the kind of time it marked was not the sort that Anne and Harry lived in. How could it be? The world was furnished with Stevens and Baudelaire — though admittedly I never found out what Anne preferred to read, supposing she did (there are people who — this is unimaginable, isn't it? — get by very well with scarcely a thought for language).

Anyway, Anne was to remain someone I never quite met. Although she came to fetch Harry several times, we were scarcely even on terms of glancing recognition when she disappeared back into the city to which she was, if anything, even more wedded than Harry was. If there was a problem, which of course there wasn't, it was that Harry was never wedded to her.

The problem was the other woman. I met her half a dozen times before I realised she *was* the other woman and not a colleague of Harry's or a friend of Anne's. Natalie would turn up in the pub or just happen to be there when we arrived. The contrast with Anne was so glaring as to be invisible, if you see what I mean. Where Anne was a pale, slight pastoral figure who should have been running a school for twelve children in the depths of Northumberland, Natalie was a creature of the city – a stilettoed blonde with crackling nylons and a voice like an icepick. Where Anne stood for patience, Natalie was all business, here, now and the next thing. Anne didn't smoke; Natalie favoured some blue-skinned, gold-tipped breed of tabs. They seemed to manufacture themselves in her tiny white handbag, into which she had evidently poured the entire contents of Wicksteeds' perfume department, where, I was not surprised to learn, she was employed in a supervisory capacity which seemed to involve standing about in a significant manner. I was only surprised that Harry should know her. She didn't strike me as a reader. Perhaps they had been at school together. Harry seemed, insofar as one could read these things, happy enough to see her. He would offer her a roll-up. She would shake her head and go on talking.

Natalie's world was full of doors she was just about to open, leading to further perfumed chambers and further exciting doors, and so on – a kind of opium dream of perpetual product launches, designed by Yves St. Laurent and Revlon. She was never stopping, only looking in, about to have to go to some unnamed but musky, darkly glittering venue. Yet her brief appearances were extremely flexible vis-a-vis the clock: Elizabeth and Helena and Coco and the rest clearly didn't mind being kept waiting. At the end of the night, when the city had once more turned into a zoo and I was aiming myself at the gaping hell-mouth of the Metro steps, Natalie would be talking about going on the Boat. The lure of this defunct cruise ship parked in the river escaped me. It has a revolving dancefloor and a legendary smell of sick. I left them to it. It is only now, in the deserts of Afterwards, that I make the connections: between Natalie and Jeanne Duval, Baudelaire's mysterious odalisque; between the local reputation of the staff of Wicksteeds' cosmetic department as part-time but vastly skilled courtesans and the cloying, imprisoning Parisian demi-monde which was the obverse of the infinite imagined ocean. Natalie was banging Harry's brains out.

Not knowing there was a crisis, I left Harry to it. Not that he would have asked for help or counsel. Not that I could have offered either. Aside from his genetic disinclination to talk about such things, our companionship was established on the basis of literary speculation. Life – that is to say, choice, responsibility, consequences – could not be permitted to intrude. That went without saying. You might object: how typically male, to overvalue – what? The pristine condition of something that in most circles would barely have qualified as conversation – *and to do so in defiance of a summons from life itself, i.e. Anne and / or Natalie*. How little you know, dear reader, if that is your view. Is there to be no space left for idleness and dreams, for the old boys' El Dorado? The Cythera of cancelled futurity?

I think, now, that Harry scarcely recognised his predicament: it was just how things went on, in the permanent meantime. But change was at hand. I noticed during the autumn that he was smoking ready-mades: Bensons, Silk Cut, nameless brands from backstreet minimarts – all of which he had previously treated with a hand-roller's studied contempt. He was lighting another before the first was finished. More than once I saw him look in disgusted bafflement at what he was smoking. How had things come to this, that life prevented him making his weekly visit to the bespoke tobacconist near the pawnbroker's shop to refurbish his supplies of Old Sumatra or Celebes Select? With the decline in the quality of smoking, so the ocean of his literary contemplations began to shrink.

There was nothing I could say. Harry's time - his world - was no longer his own, it seemed. He developed a hacking cough and struggled to mount Dog Leap Stairs on the way up from the quayside. He was often absent from the library. He altered then failed to keep drinking arrangements, or turned up very late, flustered, gasping, speechless. He staggered into the library one night, already well served by the look of him. He lowered himself into his usual seat at the big table and produced a silver hip-flask from an inside pocket. I declined the proffered shot. He emptied the flask, lit a Berkeley, put his head in his hands and said, in a voice I had never heard before, a voice from *outside* the library: 'Baudelaire's *Intimate Journals*, right? "Today I felt myself brushed by the wing of madness." I should fuckin coco. I'm fucked, man. That's the top and bottom of it. Fucked. The fuckin bitches have fuckin fucked me. Dunno where I am. Lost with all fuckin hands. Time to make smoke and disguise the heading. The Black fuckin spot's on its way.'

For a moment I was so startled I could not tell where the quotation ended and Harry began. I remember sitting there at the ashy table with my pen poised over the *TLS* crossword. This was a final leave-taking. Harry's world was being stripped of its rhetorical furnishings. All that remained was a bare unhappiness, about which there was nothing – forgive me, Tolstoy – to be said. Harry nodded, as if reading my thoughts.

'I'll catch you in the library,' he said, and walked away. Not until I heard the door swing shut did I look up. *We live, as we dream, alone.* A literary education is a wonderful thing: you need never be at a loss for the *mot juste*.

What happened next was unclear. From what I can gather, Harry went down to the quayside, though no one knows what he had in mind. It was a snowy night. It seems that when he got to an empty stretch beyond the Baltic Mill there was someone, a woman, there before him, and that this person climbed over the railings and flung herself into the river. Harry hurled a lifebelt after her, to no avail, then ran to the nearest pub to phone for the emergency services. All this I got from the barman, later.

Having made the call, Harry ordered a double and – I think a lot about this – carefully rolled himself a cigarette. He drank the whisky and smoked his tab at leisure until a siren came into earshot, after which he left the building with several other punters and stepped off the pavement, just in time to be mown down by the ambulance.

As you may imagine, I have subjected these pitiful events to lengthy scrutiny. You will understand that I have searched for evidence of order, purpose, irony, comeuppance - in short, for meaning of any kind. I have to tell you that I have made no headway whatever. The bare succeeding facts are these. The woman was never found, despite the sustained efforts of the river police. Anne and Natalie were both safe and well. Harry acquired a plate in his leg and one in his head. He is said to have renounced poetry and moved to Middlesbrough where he occupies himself in some way I have not discovered, minus the company of either woman.

What a hopeless thing a fact can be, a mere dead weight of the actual. But we must work with what we have. People. Their (eventually) obvious sadness. Apparently it must be enough to discover all merely contingent, wholly unmemorable human *mess* all over again, in papery dribs and drabs like this. Life may not amount to much: it certainly does not amount to literature, to the poems of *Harmonium* and *Les Fleurs du Mal*. Once I would kill for a book. Now I prefer to sit. I do not visit the library often, but when I do I find myself turning the pages of *Practical Photography,* wondering at the terrible unwitting power of the compliant demi-goddesses who lie in wait, there in the smoky light of those badly-imagined bordellos.

I reject this glum diminuendo! Let Harry disappear in style.

I see now that disappointment is a sort of fidelity, that for some people in some places defeat itself can be a virtue if treated with due reverence. Who is to say where disappointment springs from? But we can witness the process of its nurture all about us. The abolition of smoking in the library represents, I see now, what Harry and many others like him knew was bound to happen: not only would their ambitions be unfulfilled, their pleasures would be judged unacceptable. The world – if not Anne, then Natalie, if not her then some other damn thing – the world would be having them. The stupidity of the individual fate would be as irrelevant to this process as to everything else. One day they would look round and discover themselves to be anachronisms in a sense which had little to do with age. As a class, they were to be displaced into the realm of retired facts and foreclosed possibilities. They would take their bitterness with them as a badge of membership, but they would also have the immense, unending satisfaction of having achieved a final unshakeable immobility in which their worst suspicions were both confirmed and celebrated. Harry and his like would achieve their triumphant vindication. They would nod, roll a cigarette, exhale their smoke and vanish from sight. Harry would cease to take up the copy of *Harmonium* or Scarfe's translation of *Les Fleurs du Mal* while the great clock above the library doors unpicked the afternoon stitch by stitch. He would exit, at his own pace, from the library into nowhere, still smoking.

I have not myself smoked for many years, nor written a word till now, but with my task finished and the library at any moment about to close the doors on the world that gave it birth, I feel like lighting up just once more, for the enigmatic hell of it. *Luxe, Calme et Volupté: Tobacconists.*

# Thunder Thursday on Pemberton Grove

## J. A. Mensah

'Each door a life, each story one of a kind, each family a supernova of possibility exploding across the west end sky.'

– *Lisa Matthews*

'Invisible threads are the strongest ties.'

– *Nietzsche*

*There was nothing out of the ordinary about that day in June. It was another almost-summer's day in Newcastle. Then it happened: rainwater fell and made rivers of the streets. Pulsing through the veins of the place, it entered drains and sewers. Flowing through pipes that led to toilet bowls and kitchen sinks, it revealed unseen connections as it entered people's homes in a deluge of dirty water. The storm came, seemed like it might last forever and then vanished. But, on Pemberton Grove, the day itself had begun much like any other.*

*4am. The night was reluctant to leave. The air was cool, and streetlights peppered the road. The drawling hum of a car disturbed the peace for a moment as a taxi pulled into the street. A couple stepped out of the car. He held her face in his hands. They parted.*

No. 1: A silver number one hangs crookedly from the top centre of a pale blue door.

Becca was mortal, absolutely steaming mortal. She'd find out on Facebook in the morning what she'd been up to, but she reckoned the night had been legend! Better than anything that could have happened here. She stumbled into the house and down the corridor to her bedroom. She had the vague sense of bodies moving in the living room, but she didn't go in to see who was up. Ever since she'd stopped talking to Anne-Marie, their other housemates tret her like a pariah. They organised a house party, in the house she lived in, and didn't invite her. Well, they could go fuck themselves. She was pretty sure her night was better than theirs and she'd enjoy the rest of her second year without them looking down on her. For Becca, coming to Newcastle wasn't living it rough up North for a few years, before becoming a management consultant in yer dad's firm in London or Bristol or Wherever-upon-Avon. When you're from Ashington, coming to Newcastle is a big deal. Getting into Uni, moving out of yer family home and actually living in Newcastle, is the biggest shitting thing to happen to your family since your granddad (who worked down the mines) had that painting lesson with one of the Ashington Group. He was told if it had been a few years earlier, he could have been one of them. He was good enough to have been one of the actual Pitmen Painters. He could have had his work exhibited in Newcastle and London and in that exhibition they did in China. And that's why he pushed her so hard. He'd always known he liked to paint, but hid it from everyone and lived just sort of denying who he was.

'Just think, Becs,' he told her. 'This thing I used to hide, if I'd just talked about it sooner, showed someone, yer nah, a bit earlier, I could have been one of the Ashington Group.' His eyes glazed over as he said it, then he told her to do something with her life. And what she chose was a BA in History of Art at Newcastle University.

'What the hell do yer wanna do that for?' her mam yelled.

'What yer gonna do with that?' her dad shouted. He had this habit of only ever saying things that echoed her mum but weren't exact repetitions. He never developed a personality, is what her granddad told her about his only son. 'And when he married yer mam – well, she had so much personality, he's just sort of borrowed some of hers and hoped no one would notice.'

Before Becca could answer either of her parents, her granddad would respond, 'She's gonna make something of hersel! More than any bugger here can say. So leave the granbairn alone!'

If her granddad could see her now: living with a bunch of toffs. Their grandparents probably voted Thatcher. If he could see how she softens her accent when she's around them; elongates her a's, adding that 'aah' sound, turning words like grass and class into gr-aah-ss and cl-aah-ss. She drew the line at Newcaah-stle – she couldn't bring herself to say that. If her granddad could see her: lying half-conscious on the floor because she couldn't make it all the way to the bed, trying to remember the face of the lad that was in the back of the taxi with her, wondering what she did with him, cringing at the thought.

He'd said something to her at the end; he held her face in his hands, looked proper intense and said... she couldn't remember, her granddad's face kept interrupting. She felt like shit, and then she noticed that actual shit smell that the place always had. She wondered if Anne-Marie was somewhere in the house, feeling as terrible as she was, smelling that minging cack everywhere. Anne-Marie had been her best friend since Freshers' Week. It was the stupidest thing that they weren't talking. They'd gone out, got mortal and ended up in the Sea Nightclub on the quayside. They were on the dancefloor and the strobe lights were flashing. Becca had leaned in to say something. Anne-Marie must have thought – well, Becca didn't know what she thought, but for a minute it seemed like Anne-Marie was kissing her. The music was loud, the lights were dizzying and her head was pounding. Had she kissed Anne-Marie, or had Anne-Marie kissed her? It got really weird after that. Anne-Marie stopped talking to her and then the rest of them did too. Then Becca made it her personal mission to have sex with all the boys on her course. It didn't take long; there are only three boys in History of Art in her year. She was considering moving on to the third years and then maybe the Freshers, but only after the summer break when they'd be second years. Anne-Marie had started dating an older man. Everyone was impressed, but no one had met him. Becca was surprised when she first spotted him. He was creeping out of the house when they thought no one else was around. He wasn't a looker, a bit of a gadgie to be honest. Then the next time she saw him, sneaking out of the house again, she recognised him. He was married. With kids. And he lived at the end of the street. Anne-Marie could be a right stupid fuck sometimes.

\*

No. 5: A black metal door. The red brick of the building has been painted cream. Large areas of the paint have started to crack and fall off.

The house smelt of damp and stale smoke and had a heavy undertone of faeces. Jermaine had smelt worse, lived in worse. His cousin had said he could crash there until it was fixed up and ready for tenants. No one else in the family was talking to him, so he was grateful. The cut above his eye stung as the water hit it. He kept his face bent over the kitchen sink and carried on cleaning. His ribs ached. Each breath made them throb. He dabbed water on the cuts on his lips and tried to avoid touching the bruises and swelling elsewhere. They had left him like this, lying at the bottom of the steps that led up from the quayside to the Bridge Tavern. He couldn't say how long he'd been there, with his cheek against the concrete, watching the passing traffic beyond the alley. People walked by, on their way back from restaurants, students out clubbing midweek. They walked around him, as though he was a broken bit of the concrete steps that they had to avoid. There were a lot of dodgy steps along that way.

After Jess's death, he told himself he had to turn things around. But just because you decide to change, doesn't mean that your old life forgets you; like tonight, for example. He didn't want to dwell. But he'd also started seeing flashes of Jess – she never looked the way she had in life; she looked angry. Her face looked the way it did when he went to identify her: swollen. They said a group of teenagers had seen her floating on the Tyne and called the ambulance. Like a sponge, she'd soaked up the waters and drifted on the surface, refusing to hit the riverbed.

'Stay afloat,' she used to say. 'Never hit rock bottom, cos that's what they want you to do.' She'd said it when he quit his PhD, and again when she lost her job. She said it when they were evicted from their flat in Heaton, and again each time they moved on to something stronger. She said it the day she started calling him 'Chef': it was the first time they did heroin together. Now, the memory of her saying it was all that was left. It was that thought that got him up from the steps and out of the alley. He'd heard a girl say to the taxi driver, 'Pemberton Grove' and he felt Jess's voice between his aching ribs whispering, *stay afloat – never hit rock bottom*. He got up and staggered towards the girl and the car. She'll scream, he thought, and you'll get arrested. But that part of him that wanted to live, knew that if he stayed where he was, they would be back, and they might not leave him breathing this time. He reached for her arm. She turned to look at him. She's going to scream.

'Is he with you?' the driver asked, looking at the state of Jermaine's face.

The girl laughed and tripped backwards a little into the railings. 'I've been making a lot of new friends lately,' she slurred. 'Everybody loves Becca!' She took Jermaine's hand and led him into the taxi.

Standing at Pemberton Grove, Becca tried to pull Jermaine into her house. He looked at her through swollen eyes. Taking her face in his hands, he told her what he wished someone had told him before there were any casualties, when there was still time to do things differently. She looked up at him but didn't say anything.

As he walked into his house alone, he had a feeling that he hadn't had for years: a little less self-loathing. That night, Angry Jess didn't appear and despite the bruises, once he'd cleaned himself up, he managed to sleep.

\*

*5.15am. The morning breeze rushed along Pemberton Grove. The rising sun warmed the air and a woman in a green jacket emerged from a door and gently closed it.*

\*

No. 7: A 'No Junk Mail' sticker on a brass letterbox. A white PVC door.

Emma Wilson locked the door and walked down Pemberton Grove heading towards the General Hospital. She thought of her morning coffee and tried not to focus on the pulsing sensation at her temples. She tried not to think of that smell of poo that's getting stronger in the flat. She'd asked Matt to contact the landlord and the council. Emma had lived in Tyneside flats all her life. The West End was home: it was penny sweets from the old Woolworths on Adelaide Terrace, it was her grandparents and chasing the ice cream van after school. It was going to the pie shop and asking for pease pudding as well as mushy peas and gravy with your pie, and Granddad calling her 'soft in the head', but paying for it all the same. It was that summer when her mam said Emma should stay at her grandparents' house for the holidays, but then never came back to pick her up.

Emma had the west end of Newcastle in her veins. She knew that Tyneside flats were connected in all sorts of ways and most of them you couldn't see. She was sure that the problem with the smell in the rooms wasn't just their flat; it would be a sewerage issue affecting other houses as well. And it would keep coming back until they dealt with the whole street. Emma tried not to think that Matt wouldn't make the calls – that he'd wake up at around 2pm and start 'doing his music', and nothing else would get done. She tried not to think that it would probably be down to her to call the landlord and the council after she'd finished her 12-hour shift. The effort of trying not to think of so many things made her temples throb even more. She longed for her first fag break at 9am, when she'd bum a cigarette from one of the other nurses. She'd given up smoking but was allowed to if other people offered, that was the rule. She walked past the bakery on the West Road, where her nan used to buy bread rolls to make boiled egg stotties. A lot had changed in the area since her school days, but the old bakery was still there, and the smell of fresh bread made her stomach churn. She wasn't one to have breakfast, but that familiar, comforting scent made her think that perhaps it was time that she started.

★

*8.05am. Mr and Mrs Smith (No. 185) got into their car and Mr Green (No. 27) left to get the bus on Studley Terrace.*

*8.10am. Dr Owusu (No. 35) waited outside to be picked up by a colleague.*

*8.15am. Ms Baker (No. 59) ran to get the No. 40 bus from Westgate Road. Miss Chang (No. 47) locked her door and walked towards the town.*

*8.30am was a blur of lunchboxes, bags, gelled-hair, plaits, ponytails, and the odd toothpaste stain on a blazer. There were calls for things not to be forgotten; last-minute letters that needed signing and dinner money deposited into sticky fingers.*

*A continuous stream of cars flowed through, using the street to avoid the traffic on the main roads. Then Pemberton Grove settled.*

*4pm was a parade of rucksacks, blazers and untucked shirts, frayed plaits and broken shoelaces as the children returned from school.*

★

No. 15, A & B: Two green doors stand beside each other, uncomfortably.

No. 15A opened onto a grey carpeted staircase that led up to the Ahmeds' flat. Samira Ahmed was cleaning and cooking simultaneously. Her youngest daughter walked in from school, stamped into her bedroom and slammed the door. Samira knocked as she vacuumed outside the room. Aisha came out, looking disgruntled.
    'Will you take the washing out and hang it in the yard?'
    'Can I go out after dinner?' Aisha asked.

'Will you have finished your homework by then?'

Aisha grunted and marched past her mother. Samira told herself that she should be satisfied that at least the girl did what she was told. With no grace and very little respect, but at least she did it. If they were back home, Aisha would respect her mother, she wouldn't shout or swear at her elder sister and she would regularly speak to family members in full sentences. But Samira couldn't complain, they were lucky in many ways. They had only been in Newcastle for six years and they already had a mortgage on their own home. Saleem had been driving the taxi for three years and they were able to get the mortgage based on his salary and some savings she had. It wasn't much, a bedroom for her and Saleem, a shared room for two teenage daughters who despised each other, a small living room, a galley kitchen that led to a bathroom at the back and a little strip of yard downstairs that they accessed from a side door in the kitchen. Five rooms, a roof and a concrete strip were really all it was, but it was theirs. And she could walk out of her home and down the street to smell the spices from her mother's kitchen drifting out of occasional shops and takeaways. Once or twice a week, she'd hear people speaking her language. A few times she thought to turn around and introduce herself, invite them home to share some tea. She never did. But it was reassuring to hear their words and have that feeling of being almost at home.

Saleem emerged from the bathroom with wet hair and kissed the back of her head as he walked past her in the kitchen stirring the pot. Samira needed to find a moment to talk to him. It was about the old man downstairs. The first time she met the old man was when he knocked to complain about a leaky gutter. He explained that because the Ahmeds owned the upstairs flat, the roof and guttering were their responsibility.

She used the last of her savings to get it repaired. Then the old man knocked again and said the back gate was broken. It didn't look broken to Samira, but he'd shown her the nails that someone had been pulling out and said it would fall apart soon if it wasn't fixed.

'He's probably pulling them out himself!' Saleem had said when she told him about it later. Most of the backyard for No. 15 belonged to 15B. The Ahmeds only had a small length of the yard, but it contained the only gate by which to enter and leave, so the old man had the right to walk through their yard to exit onto the back lane. He'd told her a new gate would cost £500 and they'd had a long, inconclusive discussion about who should pay for what and if or how to split the cost. Things had gone quiet recently but then that morning, while Saleem was sleeping off his night shift, the old man came knocking. He told Samira that he and his wife, who Samira was yet to meet, own the lease to the Ahmeds' flat and they would start charging the Ahmeds a leasehold fee until the gate was fixed.

\*

The Ahmeds sat down to eat. The meal was quick and quiet. Samira was preoccupied with thinking about the old man downstairs and without her conversational prompts, her husband and daughters sat and ate in silence. Later, as the girls washed the dishes, she told Saleem about the old man and the lease. The vein in his neck throbbed as he listened. Then he got up and went to the cupboard. 'We'll talk about it later,' he said. 'That shelf in the kitchen needs fixing now.' Then he took out his toolbox and started to drill. This was becoming a habit.

In the evening when Zahra came into the living room, Samira had been staring at the document for over an hour. Zahra sat beside her mother and asked what was wrong. Her eldest daughter would be going away to university the following year and the thought made Samira's bones ache. Samira explained the old man's threat to her eldest child and showed her the deeds to the flat. Zahra took the papers and read: the words didn't seem to intimidate her. Finally, she looked up and grinned. 'Don't worry, Ma. As soon as he starts charging for the lease, we'll do the same. We've got a crossover lease; it means they own ours, but we own theirs.'

★

No. 15B: The second green door at No.15 opens beside the Ahmeds' onto a corridor that leads under their home and into the Maguires'.

The drilling had started again. The man upstairs had a habit of drilling and Alf did not like it. Nobody normal drilled that much. Alf and Rose Maguire had lived on streets off the West Road all their lives. They'd seen the West End go through a lot of changes: streets, parks, people, nearly everything that could change, had. But Alf never thought he'd see the day when he'd walk into his own home and it would smell like the Brighton Tandoori, but that smell and the drilling were constant these days.

'I think it smells nice,' Rose would say when he complained. She called herself the mediator, but that just meant she was a people pleaser who never took her husband's side. When the gutter was leaking, Rose had said to leave it, the family had just moved in upstairs, they'd probably have a lot on their plate, she'd said. But he gave them a knock anyway, had a quick word with the woman from upstairs — she was always home, never seemed to go out. Alf wondered whether she was allowed. He explained the situation to her and they sorted it out. Rose said he'd been too hasty. But there was a risk of damp and she shouldn't have to sit at home and hear the drip-drip-drip each time it rained. Rose was always out these days, at her WI meetings or volunteering at the community garden. Alf hadn't told Rose about the gate issue or the lease thing. Women don't understand some things about life, so occasionally you have to keep things from them to prevent causing undue upset. He'd tell Rose about it eventually, when it was all sorted.

The drilling from upstairs stopped suddenly. Thank the Lord. Alf rubbed his temples; his family had a history of migraines. Just as he was beginning to enjoy the calm, the bairn from next door started to howl. Bloody Tyneside flats, he thought to himself.

\*

No. 17B: A grey metal door with a black box attached to the wall beside it. The word, MAIL, has been written on it in white marker pen.

Colleen watched her five-month-old daughter nested between two pillows, dosing on the double bed. Please keep that drill going, she pleaded silently. For some reason, the only sounds that sent her little girl to sleep were fuzz, drilling, traffic – any haphazard white noise. So, in her head, Colleen begged the man from next door and upstairs to keep on drilling. She stroked the soft hairs on the little girl's head, to lure her deeper into sleep. She noticed as she did it, how much her own hand looked like her mother's. Colleen's mum had come to stay for the first month after Aoife was born. She'd gone back now, and they probably wouldn't see each other again until Christmas, and Colleen felt adrift. What if she couldn't do it properly? What if she messed up and hurt the baby by mistake? But just then, noticing how much her hand looked like her mother's, she felt calm.

The phone rang. Colleen tensed and stared at Aoife, but the baby just stirred and seemed to relax into the additional noise. Why did she even have a house phone? Colleen asked herself. He'd insisted on getting it, that's why. No one under forty had a landline phone, what was the point? The answering machine kicked in, the beep sounded: 'Col, it's me,' he said. 'Please pick up. It was a stupid mistake. You've punished me enough. Can I come home now… please?'

She couldn't forgive him. She wouldn't. She'd watched her mum forgive one worthless boyfriend after another and Colleen had promised herself that she'd be different. You had one chance, and if you betrayed her trust, that was it. He was still on the line, breathing into the answering machine, waiting for her to pick up. She crossed the room and grabbed the phone. Picking it up, she slammed it back down again, hard. The drilling stopped at the exact same time the phone connected with its cradle. Bang. Silence. Aoife started to scream.

\*

*5.05pm. Wisps of cloud huddled together then drifted apart: uncertain of whether to form. A queue of cars clotted the road.*

\*

No.57: A bright red door with a circle of frosted glass.

Chuka had the PlayStation controls in his hands and his mobile on the bed. He was Liu Kang fighting Sub Zero but also Chuka Okonkwo waiting for a message from his sort-of-girlfriend. He wasn't looking forward to it. Chuka liked Aisha, it wasn't that he didn't like her, it's just there were other things he preferred to do with his time – like playing Mortal Kombat, eating, sleeping and occasionally going to the Stanhope Halal Food Store to buy stuff from Back Home as a surprise for his mum. It made her smile and she didn't smile often. Chuka had never been Back Home but his mum said they would visit just as soon as she'd saved up enough money.

Sneaking around with Aisha had been fun at first. She'd said she'd heard that the houses on their street had attics that were connected, and they could meet and spend a night together one day in one of the adjoining lofts. It had been a very tempting offer. He hadn't been able to find the door in his attic; it was so full of stuff it was difficult to access the wall to see if a connecting door even existed.

Chuka fly-kicked Sub Zero in the chest and his nemesis bounced off the walls and the ground. After the attic failure, Aisha came up with another plan; she unscrewed parts of her backyard gate so he could squeeze his hands through the slats and let himself in. Then they would hang out in the shadows at the corner of her yard, talking about comic books and video games and people from school. They had kissed a few times too, and she let him touch inside her shirt and over the top of her bra. But it was taking up too much time. His grades had started to slip, and his mum wasn't happy when she saw his last report card. Also, Aisha was angry all the time and most of their recent conversations felt like fights. It had to end, and he hoped Aisha would understand.

Sub Zero tried to freeze him but Chuka as Liu Kang cart-wheeled out of the way. His phone beeped. He pressed pause on the game. Aisha's mum said she's not allowed out so they can't meet at Nunsmoor Park. Damn. He'd been hoping they could have the conversation somewhere public – reduce the risk of her making a scene. Another message. She suggested they meet in her backyard. He wrote back that it was too risky, they should leave it for another time.

Unpause. Back to Sub Zero. Bleep. Pause. Back to the phone. Her message said there were clothes hanging on the line and she had to go to the yard to bring them back in, no one would suspect a thing. His thumb hovered over the phone, not knowing what to write. His wrist hit 'unpause' accidentally and the game started. Sub Zero raced forward and threw a glowing blue ice ball at Chuka/Liu Kang. It crashed into his chest. Chuka lost. Sub Zero clasped his hand around Chuka/Liu Kang's neck, tightened his grip and pulled. Chuka/Liu Kang's head came off in Sub Zero's hand, with his bloody spine still attached to it. Fatality, the game crooned. It was over. Thunder roared outside Chuka's bedroom window. He thought better of breaking up with Aisha today.

★

*5.32pm. The clouds formed, greyed and indicated their intentions.*

Becca at No. 1 woke up and everything hurt: her head was pounding and her stomach felt like it was going through a meat-grinder. Her period had started earlier, and the pain had woken her up. She'd dragged herself off the bedroom floor and into the bathroom. As she sorted herself out, she'd noticed that a wrapped sanitary towel was already in the bin. Someone else was riding the crimson wave. She'd put money on it being Anne-Marie. Their menstrual cycles had synchronised within a couple of months of living together. Becca lay on the bed thinking about it and it felt like a strange intimacy – inside, their bodies were moving to the same rhythm, while in the outside world, they weren't even talking. Outside her door, she heard Anne-Marie's hushed giggle and another voice. Becca pulled a pillow over her head: Anne-Marie was sneaking the old gadgie from down the road into the house. Minging.

Jermaine at No. 5 lay on his bed staring at the ceiling, trying to get back that feeling from last night, that sense of being almost OK.

*There was a rumble of hooves from the air.*

Emma Wilson left her shift at the General Hospital and started to make her way to No. 7 Pemberton Grove.

Samira Ahmed (No. 15A) kissed her husband and waved him goodbye from the door. Saleem got into his car ready to start his shift. There was a storm coming; that should be good for business, he thought.

Alf (No. 15B) peeked outside the window and hoped Rose would come home soon.

*The sky turned black. Lightning flashed. Rain began to fall.*

Baby Aoife (No. 17B) drifted to sleep to the sounds of the storm. Colleen lay beside her. If he called again, she might pick up.

Chuka (No. 57) text Aisha to say they shouldn't meet in the rain. No shit Sherlock, she text back.

*It rained hard and the downpour ran off the town moor and flowed through the streets. Clouds burst; thunder boomed; there was a flash, and lightning struck the Tyne Bridge.*

Becca remembered what that lad from last night had said and it gave her the sudden urge to call her granddad.

Jermaine noticed that there was water seeping into his room from the bottom of the door. He closed his eyes tight. He was hallucinating, for sure.

Emma walked through the downpour and marched straight past her house. She wasn't concerned about Matt; he could look after himself, and if he couldn't, it was about time he learned.

Samira watched live weather updates on TV, she saw the bolt from the sky hit the Tyne Bridge. It looked like a disaster movie.

Alf sat in the flat below Samira, watching BBC Look North. Carol Malia was on. Alf liked her; she'd been on Look North for years. Alf liked her consistency. She talked about flooded streets, blocked roads and how the Metro was off. 'The advice at the moment is to stay in higher rooms and apartments,' Carol said. Living in a one-bed, ground floor flat didn't offer that option to Alf. He would have expected more practical advice from Carol. He wondered where Rose had got to; she'd better be getting home soon.

*The street was a swirling mass of dirty water. A manhole cover blew off and a volcano of filth erupted.*

Hopefully, that will be the end of the shitty sewerage issue, Emma thought as she avoided the brown spray from the manhole and waded towards 15B. She banged on the door of the house, 'Granddad. Granddad!'

'Rose? Rose? Is that you?' Alf asked as he opened the door.

'Granddad, it's me, Emma. Nan's dead, remember?' Emma pushed her way in and closed the door. The rain had already made its way into the flat. The carpet was under inches of water and Emma couldn't see where it was coming from. She started to think through their options. She couldn't take him back to her place, it was also on the ground floor. There was a knock on the door.

'That'll be Rose,' her grandfather said.

Emma opened the door to see a woman standing outside. She was wearing an orange headscarf and holding a blue umbrella.

'I'm Samira Ahmed, I live upstairs,' she said. 'I wanted to

check if…' Samira realised she didn't know the old man's name. 'I wanted to check if he was OK, if he needed anything.'

'I'm perfectly fine,' Alf said. 'Goodbye now.'

Samira looked down at the drenched carpets, paused and then suggested they all go upstairs to wait the storm out in her home. 'It's just me and my daughters up there at the moment. You can dry your feet and have a warm cup of tea.'

Becca came off the phone to her granddad in Ashington and she felt better. So much better that even the cack smell of the house seemed like it was fading. Her granddad was surprised by her call. Yes, she was fine. Was he OK? He was fine. She told him what she'd been up to, an edited version. He listened. She told him she was living with people who were probably Tories. He wasn't angry. She told him she wasn't speaking to her best friend. He said that when he was young, they sometimes wrote letters when things were difficult to say. It was daft and old-fashioned, but she thought she might give it a go.

Jermaine stood on the bed watching the water rising on the ground. Was it real? Was he seeing things? The water was creeping towards the bed and there was a figure in the doorway. He tried to ignore them both. Stay afloat. Stay afloat, he said, trying to calm his mind. He remembered the girl from last night, what he'd told her. With his whole body shaking, he tried to take his own advice: he forced himself to turn and look at Jess. The skin on her face was puckered and grey but her big dark eyes were the same as they'd been in life: mesmerising. His eyes stung as the tears came, 'I'm sorry,' he told her. She looked calm. Stay afloat, she said, but for real this time.

Emma sat with her granddad, Alf, inside the Ahmeds' home as Samira added cloves and cardamom to the tea on the cooker.

# THUNDER THURSDAY ON PEMBERTON GROVE

Outside the thunder rumbled.

'Thunder spoils milk,' Alf said. It was something Rose used to say.

'Not condensed milk,' Samira replied as she poured the tin of Carnation into the pan.

Emma smiled, she liked Samira. When Samira brought the cups of steaming tea to them, it smelt like Christmas. Alf had started talking about Rose again, as though she were still alive. The doctor had advised Emma to join in the conversation but to speak of her grandmother in the past tense to help her grandfather get used to his loss.

'My nan used to say, about Tyneside flats, that they're all knotted together.'

Samira laughed and nodded, 'Before moving into this place, I would never have believed it if someone had told me!'

Alf drank his tea quietly as his granddaughter continued to mention his wife in the past tense. It sounded strange. Another change in the West End that he was being forced to get used to. But the tea tasted quite nice, though it wasn't his usual. And he liked the sound of Samira's laugh. It was the first time he'd heard it. He watched as his granddaughter talked to Samira, the woman from upstairs. She wasn't Rose, but besides Our Emma, she was the only other person Alf spoke to these days.

## Author's Note

On 28th June 2012, a storm that lasted two hours caused flash flooding in Newcastle upon Tyne. Lightning struck the Tyne Bridge, there were power cuts to 23,000 homes, and trains north of the city were cancelled after a landslide on the tracks. A report commissioned by Newcastle City Council estimated that the storm caused £8 million of damage to homes, roads and businesses.

# Living on Planet Clacky

## Glynis Reed

DURING THE WEEK, CLACKY wanted to be Tinkerbell, but on Saturday's she was a Tiller Girl, entertaining us with high kicks and Mam's too-big stiletto heels and pink sparkly cut-down dress. Mam said Clacky was destined for the stage, Gran said she was Doris Day and Audrey Hepburn rolled into one, Dad said she was a fairy, and me? I knew she was a star and a wonder and everything I wasn't.

I was bald until I was three and when my hair did grow, it grew sludge brown and poker straight, but Clacky was born with hair, the kind that twinkled and twisted and curled itself around your fingers, and enhanced her pretty face and big green eyes. She had teeth too, although she wasn't born with them. They just appeared one day, shining like smooth, white Christmas lights, and growing cute and straight, and making mine look like horse's teeth.

The truth is, I felt like a horse next to Clacky. She was dainty and wore everything well, even my old cast-offs (I was three years older and money was tight on account of Dad's glass back) and it puzzled me that I didn't look as good in my clothes when they were new as Clacky did after I'd worn and outgrown them.

When Mam sent us to the shop for hot, just-baked buns,

we'd stop several times cos Clacky attracted people. They'd ask her name and age, and stare at her, as if they were fixing her in their memory. But Clacky wasn't aware of the effect she had on others; she'd just answer their questions and shine her big dreamy eyes at them while I hugged the warm buns and watched her, and felt proud of her, and loved her, even more than they did.

Dad often said she wasn't made for this world. He'd waltz her round on his curly feet and ask her when she was going to fly away. And Clacky would look serious and hold his big smiling face in her patient hands and tell him, again and again, that she could only fly at night, in her dreams.

I don't know why Dad stopped loving Mam but he did and she knew it. We could tell by her face, how the corners of her mouth resembled the twists on our two-ounce bags of rainbow drops, and how her eyelids got sad, and startled, and careful, especially when Dad was larking about with Bella Bristles, who lived at the top of our street.

We called her Bella Blot, cos that's what she was, a big, blowsy blot. All twice-baked meringue hair and clever eyebrows, and the kind of walk that made you think of the pistons on steam engines.

Clacky complained that her chest hurt, and mine did too, and it suddenly bothered me that Dad always called me Big Aggie. But Clacky, who was already tiny, got tinier and very quiet, the sort of quiet where you know there's lots going on inside. I could hear her brain whirring like Mam's twin-tub, and she started having nightmares.

I'd wake to her creeping into my bed, pressing herself into the folds of my nightie and crying about the face that was like a big sheet with huge eyes and a huge mouth, that she couldn't stop herself flying into. In the morning, I'd be helping Mam with breakfast and we'd hear Clacky shouting that someone was under the bed, waiting to grab her ankles. She'd run into the kitchen and there we'd be, Mam and the hamster, and the fire and me, all busy roasting and toasting and trying to make things safe, just for her.

Mam paid the bills by working at the bakery. We hadn't seen Dad since he'd run off with Bella Blot, until we saw him up a tree in the *Chronicle* rescuing a cat. 'Felix Christens Local Hero,' it said. And it's true, there was the cat, squirming in Dad's hand. He was grinning nervously as it drenched him in a shining, liquid, arc of relief.

That was the day Clacky got parky about the school's diarrhoea mince and horsehair potatoes and we started having lunch at home, so Mam could praise her for eating. And Gran brought seed cake, and talked about people with nothing to eat, and about being twelve and having toothache, and going to the Dentist and carrying a bag of coal. My thighs, which never got praised, were eyeing the seed cake but I was thinking about *The Little Match Girl,* and wondering where Gran put the coal while the Dentist examined her teeth. But when I looked at Clacky, she was looking at babies, with light bulb heads and still faces, and big eyes and big bellies, that were looking at us, from the telly.

She started playing the wag, haunting bus stops, and hanging around with kids from the estate. Coming in late with glazed eyes and a Babycham tongue, trapping Mam's voice in the door till Mam pleaded with her, and cuddled her, and called her a little fairy and hit her with a number ten knitting needle, for her own good, and cos she didn't want her getting hurt.

And I'd try to sleep while Clacky sat on the bed with her small, sharp, shoulder blades nudging her sweater, like defeated wings. And I'd go to school with Mam and sit next to her, while Miss Cuthbertson breathed heavily and mentioned Clacky and lost days and lost potential, and girls who should be flying – and I'd hold Mam's hand and concentrate on her knuckles, and wish Clacky's sharp little shoulder blades *would* turn into wings, so she could fly away.

Mam and I gradually accepted that Dad had a new family, probably with curly feet and burgeoning bristles. It said so in the paper, that he had twin boys, I mean, not that they had bristles. We just didn't know how to tell Clacky that some dads are feckless and want things to be new all the time – even their children!

But I couldn't articulate the words cos I didn't know them, or have time to think about them, cos I was worried about leaving school, and not having new clothes, or Calvados tights, and I didn't even know myself if it's true about dads being feckless.

I just wanted her to settle down and be normal or at least pretend to be normal, until I got things out of the way, like work, and tights, and earning money and finding friends, cos although I was never gonna be a fairy, I thought starting work might give me a chance to leave Big Aggie behind me.

But Clacky had to pull that stunt on the bridge, because she'd bumped into Dad and 'Bella Blot' and their new family. At least that's how it started. I knew she was sensitive, some people are, extraordinarily so, but I was sick of her living on Planet Clacky all the time and she should have known I didn't mean it.

I just told her to come down to Earth and stop worrying Mam. And I told her she was selfish, and I said that, about her being selfish, till I lost count of the times. And I told her Dad wasn't coming back. And I didn't let it bother me that she had that closed, tight look. I just went on and on till she put her hands over her ears and ran to the bridge in the middle of Jesmond Dene, and got up on the rail and stood there, like when we stood on the pavement at the edge of the kerb and held our noses and said: 'I'm gonna jump – goodbye, cruel world!'

And it was just like Clacky, that she could look great, standing on the rail of the bridge without wobbling, in the middle of autumn, with the leaves glowing, and touching and sighing round her. It didn't even matter that her nose was red, or that she had her platforms on, and her red loons, cos someone had painted a crown on her head that was gold, and red, and green and umber. And the leaves kept falling from the trees, burning and shimmering on her back, and I knew Dad was right, and that Clacky really was a fairy.

I wanted to say I was sorry, but a crowd had gathered, and dogs were rooting through the leaves, and the leaves were crackling, and some had the flesh torn off them so you could see the fragile, skinny skeletons that held them together. Then a man in a knitted hat with a dodgy bobble shouted: 'Don't move, I'll come and get you.'

And he put his bag down cos he was that type of man, who did his own shopping with a shopping bag, and bought fresh bread, and had big hands and a soft face and got called 'Mary'. But I could tell that Clacky wasn't listening to him, or looking at him, and I forgave her, for being everything I wasn't. Because I knew then, that everything was going to be alright for Clacky and that she was just going to see Tinkerbell, and live in Neverland, with the lost children, cos I could see her pretty face, it was flying towards me, and it was smiling.

# The Here and Now

## Margaret Wilkinson

THERE'S BAD NEWS FROM the doctor. You walk quickly, probably trying to prove something to yourself. Then inevitably become breathless. At home, you make a pot of coffee and drink two cups. You want everything to be ordinary, but nothing is. In a fit of rage, you tear up your diet sheet. For the first time in years, you want a smoke. You find a near empty pack of stale Marlboro Lights. Open the window facing the cemetery. Very appropriate under the circumstances. Light up. Look out. Cough.

Westgate Hill Cemetery is filled, day and night, with drunks and junkies. Rubbish accumulates between the gravestones, many of which are broken or marred with graffiti. Beer cans, needles, condoms, plastic carrier bags, deflated footballs. You shake your head. The legendary chapel of rest has been demolished. The gates and boundary rails carried away for other purposes. Everything moves on. Obviously. Still a shame. One of the first garden cemeteries in England, built in 1829. Well, you live in the neighbourhood so ought to know. You signed the petition complaining about overgrown vegetation and anti-social behaviour.

Today a group of people dressed in black snake between the derelict headstones and broken masonry. They are led by a figure wearing a cape and a cleft hat. Imagine that! Six men stagger under the weight of a dark wood coffin. Are you sure? You lean out the window. It's a long way down. You didn't even know the cemetery was still in use. Last burial 1957, you find when you google. Has it reopened?

It's November and the days are short. It seems morbid to schedule a funeral so late in the afternoon, but you're intrigued. Maybe it's a staged re-enactment. Maybe Goths, you think.

That night you order a Domino's stuffed crust, Mighty Meaty with extra cheese, and open a cold bottle of Newcastle Brown. You tap a drumroll on the table. Start to whistle. Kick back. This is what it's all about. Pizza. Dog. Put on the telly. Flick through the channels. Carelessly pop a heart pill. End up watching an old American detective series. A psychic with an identical twin predicts her sister's death by strangulation.

Finish the pizza. Finish the Dog. Listlessly get out your calculator and do some sums for work. Then listen to a CD you like. While listening, you feel a welling in your chest and begin to cry. Although it's still early, you're tired. Tiredness is a symptom of your illness. Now that's not fair, is it?

Feeling as if you've swallowed masonry, and vowing never to order Domino's again, you check the window before turning in. A grave digger carrying a spade leans against the cemetery wall (sandstone, Grade II, listed) and lights a pipe. You can't remember the last time you saw anyone smoke a pipe. The point of his spade defined by the glare of the high-pressure sodium lamps that line the road. The rest of the cemetery stretching away into darkness.

It's only eight o'clock, but you get into bed and immediately fall asleep. Dream you're cycling down the smooth, steep incline on Bishop's Road, or Ethel Street, or

## THE HERE AND NOW

Atkinson Road – that was a good one – in Benwell, behind your childhood home. Feel the wind rush past your ears. When you open your eyes, the room is dark as a crypt.

This is the last good night sleep you will have. *Behold*, you think like a lunatic, *I show you a mystery. We shall not all sleep, but we shall all be changed, in a moment, in the twinkling of an eye.*

This is you. Once a fit bloke. Going slack around the middle. Your nearly hipster beard patchy in places.

Only thirty-six years old. You know. It's shite. Even worse than that. You need surgery. The operation will be risky, and you've told the consultant at the Freeman you require a few days to think. Without the op, your condition will worsen, but you can't commit. 'I will not lie to you,' the consultant said. He's a middle-aged man with a square, healthy face that's just showing jowls. During your frequent consultations, you have formed an unfavourable impression of him. While he speaks, you count the diplomas on his wall. For a moment you fear you might cry, but you take it like a man. As if from a great distance, you hear the words bypass surgery, valve replacement, angioplasty, vasodilator, nitro-glycerine, Demerol, heart failure. The word 'failure' upsets you.

'What do you want to do?' the doctor asks.

You want to hit him.

Next day you go to work as usual. Hold tight to the bannister and pant slowly down the stairs. In the hall, you nod to a neighbour. Your chest hurts too much to speak. A chill wind blows down Elswick Road (formerly Elswick Lane) on one side of the cemetery where you wait for the number 30, 31, 32 or 32A. A lane is not a road you think, imagining trees, bluebells, horses. Once upon a time, there were wrought-iron palisades on top of the cemetery walls. Your nan doesn't even remember that.

You could afford to live elsewhere. Maybe. But what's the point now? Besides, there's all the familiar things. The air clear, clean-ish, cold. Morning sun flaring. Long, wide sweeping views at this end of the town. A lot of Northern sky which always makes you feel inquisitive, keyed up, alive. The busy road, the slits between houses, narrow empty side streets, worn stone. Even the sour damp smells off the river. And the unfamiliar things. The Kurdish restaurant, Bengali Express; Turkish hair, Halal meat. The languages and faces.

On the bus, a girl offers you her seat. You're not going far. You used to walk it. But feeling so fragile, you sit. At your stop, you have to be helped off by another kind passenger. When he sets you down, you tremble like a leaf. Pulling yourself together, you grump off.

You own an ecologically-friendly bike shop. It's a fairly new business, started before your health began to fail. You sell micro-shell helmets, rear-fitting pannier bags, Lycra gear, child seats, speedometers, front and rear krypton lights, U-shaped shackle locks, water bottles, mini-pumps, as well as top-of-the-range and made-to-order cycles with a wide variety of gears. You're in debt up to your eyeballs but your work pleases you. You love bicycles. Their simple logic. The way they fit together. The chain transmitting motion from the pedals to the wheels. Although you have not been on one in years. Not since your condition was first diagnosed. Last time you rode you went right over the handlebars. Whack. Thud. Out. You were fine before that. Heart-wise. That accident started everything. Think about it.

Your employees stop talking and turn their heads to look at you. You have two salesmen out front with wind-hardened faces from riding in all weathers. In the back, your assistant and a mechanic are drinking coffee. Both steroid-boosted, road racing fanatics. Leg muscles like boulders. You could hate them all.

## THE HERE AND NOW

Instead, you shake hands. A classic chop from the top. You swallow a shaky glug of coffee. Want to appear fit but you've been breathless for months, stumbling vacantly, diminished in height. They all think flu. Or maybe they know. They've got to know.

Clients ring up to find out how their custom-made bikes are progressing.

Slowly.

It's one of those days.

Reminding yourself to live in the here and now, you resolve to notice the things around you, but your mind cannot help racing backwards and forwards in time so you see nothing of the present. The future, in particular, dominates your thinking. You have always felt that if you plan ahead, down to the smallest detail, everything will be okay. Is that not rational? Logical? You have spent much of your life planning, which is why you have little experience living.

You're a dead man.

You shuffle up the road towards home trying to hide your gently sloping, then steeply sloping walk. Should have called a taxi. When you pass the cemetery, you notice the wrought iron gates you saw yesterday from your window are gone again.

'Here and now,' you say, trying to remind yourself to live in the moment. You worry you will forget. It's a fine late afternoon. Clear and already frosty. 'Here and now,' you repeat, blocking out the street, the weather, the enamel sky, the neighbours, the couples, the groups of lads ready to kick off, the dogs.

'Here and now.'

When you get home, you write these three words down in an otherwise blank notebook. Imagining the circuits of your heart tree-lined and gently curving, you try to relax.

That evening, you go to the window, gaze out at the stars. You feel all right considering. In the cemetery below, there's another procession, snaking between the gravestones. Goths. This time you're certain.

Some years back, grave robbers plundered the old family crypts in the cemetery below your window. Undisturbed for one hundred years. It's the truth. Your dad read it in the *Evening Chronicle* in 1984. You can still find it online. Using pickaxes and shovels, they dug their way underground. When the police arrived, they tried bolting. Five members of a ritual-industrial-improv-goth project band inspired by Tibetan music. Lads, really. Using plundered bones to make their instruments.

The window is double glazed and only muffled sounds reach you, but you think you hear a drum beat. And a thin reedy sound that could be produced by blowing into bones. Tibetan leg flutes as they are called. You've done your research. Traditionally made from human femurs. Producing a sound in the West End of Newcastle like the singing of elephants.

You should ring the police. But for some reason, you get down on your knees in front of the window and remain there until you become stiff. Femurs aching.

The femur, or thigh bone, has a round head at one end where it fits into the pelvic bone forming the hip joint and a smaller protuberance at the other end where it joins the knee. Holes are made on both sides of the knee – the blowing end – turning the bone into a musical instrument. Reputed to have healing powers, female bones are said to produce a clearer sound. Men's more like an edgy whistle. Children, unthinkable mewing.

If the consultant rings you're not in. You're out.

Your girlfriend Rachel wants you to have the op. That evening, she comes downstairs to see you. She lives in the same block of flats. Vallum Court. Also known as Valium Court, naturally. It's how you met. What's a vallum? You have no idea. The huge defensive ditch, the no-man's-land, dug by the Romans, outside Hadrian's Wall, which once ran right down Westgate Road.

Well, what else is Google for?

Rachel, a generous mouth, lots of teeth, high gums, a complicated face, wears vintage clothes. Her hair, tonight in an unusual style, is rolled back from her forehead. On other occasions, hair in tangles, she wears white Victorian lace faded to lemon. She is the part-owner of a pop-up shop in Fenham called HOW IT WAS that sells these types of garments.

'A funny thing's been happening,' you say to her. You take her to the window to show her the cemetery. Run your fingers across the glass. 'I like the idea of a resting place,' you say, pointing. 'That would be a nice spot.'

'You're joking,' she laughs.

Two drunks below start arguing. A beer bottle is thrown, and you find you no longer wish to converse, seized by a pain in your chest. Rachel kicks off her shoes and sprawls gracefully in a chair. Then she gets up and puts her arms around you. You've been together years. She can't leave now. Can she? Your own emotions, buried six feet from the surface and sprinkled with quick lime, are not for sharing. You pick up a copy of *Bicycling News Today* and pretend to read.

After she leaves, you think about it. You're a sensible bloke. You go to the window and stare down at the cemetery again. It looks like a ruin. You take off your glasses, wipe the lenses. You've been in an agitated state. Your brain is not getting enough oxygen. You've been warned about this very thing.

Before bed, you eat a large bag of cheddar and red onion crisps. You are not sure it is worth living without them. *Death is swallowed up,* you think. That night, lying in bed, you hear the echoing tread of men dragging around a heavy object.

Next time you walk past the cemetery, you decide to enter. It's been a windy day, but inside the air is still. The light is brighter, more golden. The smell of wood smoke and softly rotting leaves reminds you of childhood. It's odd, living where you do, that you've never been inside the cemetery before. Not too bad, once you pass through the gates. Quiet. Peaceful.

A large floral spray is propped against a small grey stone, almost obscuring it. You bend to read the card. *Dearest Minerva – You are always in our hearts – Love Arthur, Serena and Sidney.*

You straighten up and realise you are not alone. In fact, the cemetery is full of visitors. They gather, on their own or in small groups, around weeping archangels, obelisks and marble vaults.

Where are the beer cans, shredded tights, dog turds? Perhaps a benefactor with deep pockets has been found. An angel. In the distance, you notice a woman standing in front of a piece of granite, carved in the form of a broken column. She wears a long dark skirt and a jacket shaped to the waist, flaring further down, like something Rachel would wear.

You wander for a while, feeling quite content in the golden light, shifting your head from side to side. When you become tired you sit on a commemorative bench. The soil at your feet a rich moist brown, like Christmas pudding. Before you, a Gothic monument inlaid with marble. A low relief of Jesus wearing flowing robes, and the motto: I WAS SICK AND YE VISITED ME, pierced by gilded darts of light.

A group of gardeners in flat caps wave as they set off whistling, tools slung over their shoulders. A bit awkwardly, you wave back. Birds flit from stone to stone. Watching them, you feel very light and your heavy breathing is, for a time, eased. You feel happy in the here and now. Then, because you can't help it, you begin to plan.

'I want to see about purchasing a plot,' you say to an old man who emerges from the tiny, crypt-shaped building that you take to be the cemetery lodge, purportedly demolished in 1970 along with the chapel of rest.

'Certainly,' he says. 'Follow me.'

Dainty and wizened, he reminds you of your maternal grandfather. He leads you into a small, bare room. In one corner there's a desk and two chairs. In the other, a polished oak coffin half-covered with a pall is displayed on a stand. 'They aren't cheap these plots. But it's a restful place. Money well spent,' the little man murmurs, turning to face you.

Glass crunches beneath your feet.

'You'll have to pardon the condition of the building. We've had a break-in.' He shows you where the outer door has been forced and shakes his head. 'Is this plot for yourself, sir? Or someone else?'

'Myself,' you say.

'I see. Then you wouldn't want a double?'

'A double?'

'Not married then?' He sits down behind his desk with a pleasant expression and motions you towards the chair that's facing him. Someone (the intruder) has thrown grit or dust over everything.

'No.' You collapse gratefully. 'I'm not married.'

'Are you thinking of getting married? You've got to plan ahead in these matters. It wouldn't do for you to be buried here, the wife left out in the cold, as it were.'

'I'll just take the single for now,' you say.

'Eight hundred pounds,' he says. 'Cash.'

You raise your head. 'Eight hundred pounds?' You pull at your fingers nervously. 'In cash?'

'Everyone wants a place like this.' He touches his breast pocket. 'I could give you a special price on a double. A double for twelve.'

You'll have to go away and think about it. Maybe make some arrangements.

*What is there to think about,* you say to yourself. The alternative is cremation, spending eternity on Rachel's mantelpiece, or at the back of her wardrobe with her old shoes.

'Come in person. We're not on the phone.' He rises from his chair and strides towards you. Up close he doesn't look as affable as your granddad. 'It's a prime site. They're going fast.'

You close your eyes for a minute. When you open them, he's busy tidying his desk, brushing dust into his hands.

'This is really a unique offer.' His eyes twitch. 'The council has reopened the cemetery for a limited time only.'

The idea's crazy. All your cash is tied up in the shop. Yet you think of nothing else as you stumble home. It's a privilege. Imagine all the important people buried there. Public benefactors, surgeons, academics, prominent manufacturers from a hundred years ago or more. You'll be joining them. Well-to-do people. Victorians. Men with monocles and dressed hair, long-faced and appropriately grim; women who breed ponies; toffs who lived in big houses with columns and mirrors and fine furniture; innocent children in tiny shoes with buckles, dead from hives and glands; lads on penny-farthing bicycles bought for them by indulgent fathers; corseted girls; old soldiers; fifteen recorded World War I casualties; veterans of the first Anglo-Afghan War, the Crimean War. It is as if a gate or boundary in your mind has been removed and you skip down a steep semi-circular embankment, whooping.

## THE HERE AND NOW

Rachel rings and asks if you've phoned the consultant yet. She does not understand why people dither, become fretful, or depressed. Why they weep, lose hope. Why they laugh or cry when reading a book, watching a film, or listening to music. She has a very positive, practical attitude and is at her best in waiting rooms or hospitals.

Instead of ringing the consultant, you have an online chat with your bank.

After you buy a plot from the old gent, for £800, you receive an onionskin document confirming the purchase. 'Is this all the proof I'll need when the time comes?'

'You got it,' he says, squeezing your shoulder.

Once your deal's concluded, he puts on his coat. 'I must leave you now. But take your time. Look around.'

'That's all right.'

You think you might go home and phone the consultant, tell him to go ahead and plan your op. It will please Rachel. And if things go wrong, you have your resting place.

You need to get home. Tired, you begin to stagger, lurching through the cemetery. You can't help it. You have a condition. Your heart labours and you gasp for breath. Putting a hand to your chest, you're alarmed by the thumping you feel. Blurred shapes streak past spinning circles of light. The tiny white pill nearly slips from your grasp.

The following week, you decide to ask Rachel to marry you. Your operation is scheduled. You think it's a good moment to get engaged. If you die on the table, Rachel will probably feel better about having made a meaningful commitment. If you survive, your marriage will be a celebration. *And the dead shall be raised incorruptible*, you think. You want to take her to the cemetery to ask her. If she agrees, you'll save to buy her a plot too. Convert your single into a double.

Opening the wardrobe, you take out a shirt with French cuffs. You dress with care. In the bedroom mirror, the whites of your eyes are grey, but you look good. You step into your continental trousers. Now you look like an undertaker. No you don't. You look like a corpse. You have a whisky to calm those nerves. What if she says no? You hold the bottle with both hands and glug.

Rachel has no idea of your romantic intentions. She holds your arm as you walk down the road. You're impatient to get inside, but she refuses to enter. 'Are you crazy?' she asks. 'We'll be mugged.'

'Nonsense,' you say and drag her through the stone piers on Westgate Road (formerly Arthur's Hill Road). The lodge is a ruin, you see that now. The floral tributes are gone, instead a drift of dead leaves. The headstones overgrown with moss and weeds. Flattened. Shattered. Defaced. Askew. No swept paths. No bird song. The grass has not been maintained. Rubbish everywhere. The blackened remains of an old fire, one high heeled shoe, a bent iron bar, a sour smell. All that, and a drunk waving his arms in the air. 'I'll chop you one,' he cries.

'How long do we have to stand here?' Rachel picks up a fallen leaf, rubs it to pieces angrily between her fingers, releasing a strong, sharp smell. Urine. She drops it and runs.

'Rachel, wait!'

You shake your fist at the tumbled down lodge. You've been conned. 'Those buggers in old-fashioned clothes,' you holler. 'I want my money back!'

On the road outside, pure fury. You, gasping for breath, sinking to your knees, grabbing onto a small drinking fountain set into the outer wall on Elswick Road (1859, Grade II, listed). The basin full of crap.

## THE HERE AND NOW

Rachel helps you take a pill. You feel the blood pumping weakly around your body. The hair on your head is damp.

'Let's go home,' she says her voice tinny and far away.

'I've been had,' you croak stupidly as you turn onto Westgate Road. You want to tell her to stop holding you so tight. She's crushing your arm, but you can no longer speak.

A black horse-drawn carriage pulls up beside you. You note it briefly. A man in a top hat emerges. Sensing the flow of life ceasing, you can see yourself lifted now, floating, then soaring back, through the cemetery gates and down the gravel path that glows in a tunnel of light.

# Blood Brothers

## Jessica Andrews

WHEN WE WERE SPLATTERED with freckles and tied up in pigtails, we picked sharp rocks from the garden and pushed them into each other's wrists, our flesh tender and white like peeled crabs. I remember the way our wounds looked, mushy and filled with pieces of grit.

'Now we are blood brothers,' I said. She looked at me from behind her nose.

'Blood *sisters*,' she pouted.

We got changed on the back seat of the car every Wednesday night as my mam drove us from school to our dance class, held in a cold room above a chip shop on the Chilli Road. We fumbled our way into fishnets and slurped purple Ribena from plastic cartons, comparing the clusters of keyrings on our matching backpacks. She was smaller than me, so she always got picked to play the best parts, like being lifted into the air by teenage boys in flared Lycra. My mam sat late into the night sewing sequins onto our leotards, ruining her cuticles to make our small bodies glitter as we flitted across the stage.

We grew out of green gingham summer dresses and frilly hair bobbles, into sparkly butterfly clips and bubblegum lip gloss.

My parents got divorced and my mam held my hand while a lady smelling of sunbeds pushed cubic zirconia into my navel. Her parents stayed together and she put a stainless-steel bar through her nipple in secret. She got on the school bus first in the mornings and listened to Destiny's Child on her iPod Mini until she got to my stop. I would claim the seat in front of her, crossing my legs so the glittery nail varnish on my pink Converse caught the light. We spoke mostly in code and giggled through our braces all the way to registration.

We streaked each other's hair with purple dye and took to wearing our dads' old T-shirts torn at the necks. We spent Saturday afternoons ogling people we knew from Myspace on Goth Green, sharing bottles of White Lightning and watching the skaters in Exy Park, desperate for them to notice us in our cut-up Ramones T-shirts. We stumbled up the stairs of Northumbria Union on school nights, thrilled by the bare backs brushing our bellies beneath our crop tops. We smeared red eyeshadow across our lids for My Chemical Romance and asked The Hives to sign our knickers.

'How *old* are you?' They worried in their white suits, pressing their Sharpies into our bum cheeks.

Someone made us friendship bracelets out of special beads that changed colour in the sunlight. We labelled them 'virgin bracelets' and, one after the other, we cut them off with shaking hands and kitchen scissors. We stopped eating lunch and started applying fake tan. We went to the back room of a beauty salon in Walkergate and stood together, stark naked, as a woman sprayed our bodies with orange liquid from a long hose.

'Lift your arms up,' she barked, and we did, in unison, 'so you don't get white bits under your pits.'

Newcastle seemed small and we felt full of possibility. We zipped each other into bandage dresses and blagged our way into Gotham to drink treble vodka oranges, piling our leather jackets in a corner as we croaked the Oasis dawn chorus on the sticky dancefloor. We twirled in damp circles to The Smiths at Jukebox, losing our phones and bruising our thighs on the stairs as we toppled over in our platform shoes. Once, we both passed out on a chip shop floor, and a taxi driver carried us into his cab and drove us home.

I fell in love with a boy at school who wore bangles and wooden beads, and did his eyeliner in the toilets at lunchtime. We went to parties at his house in Birtley, where people swallowed his sister's Ritalin and had sex in the alleyways. One night, a police officer knocked on the door while we were jumping on the settee in our spangled dresses.

'Do you mind if we have a quick look around?' he asked us. There had been armed police lining the high street for days because a man called Raoul Moat had shot his ex-girlfriend in a house down the road and was on the run. We didn't even pretend to be sober.

'Sure, mate,' my boyfriend winked, 'but I don't think you'll find him in here.'

My boyfriend and I shared bottles of rosé wine in the Dog & Parrot after school, putting Milburn on the jukebox and snogging on the cracked leather sofas. We jumped the Metro and skulked around South Shields, running naked into the freezing sea. We carved our names into the 100-year-old lifeboat displayed on the seafront and stole Fanta from the Subway self-service machines. She started going dancing without me, applying false eyelashes and skittering across the Diamond Strip in a pair of Kurt Geiger's. She sat in the passenger seat of second-hand Nissan Micras, mouthing the words to Beyoncé songs and drawing her eyebrows on in the rear-view mirror.

I stopped drinking Diet Coke by the canal with her at lunchtime and began going to the sixth form library to scribble essays, a different kind of life growing beneath my eyelids. She spent her free periods with boys who lived nearby and turned up to Media Studies wearing their boxer shorts underneath her trousers. She invited me for chips at the Tanners after college, but I turned her down to eat cheese toasties in my boyfriend's bed.

I got a place at university and packed everything I owned into an enormous grey suitcase. The night before I left, we went out dancing together for the last time. She wore a silver dress and flickered like lightning beneath the strobe lights. Later, my new friends would make fun of the way I'd trailed strange bits of miscellany across the country, like used envelopes and clumps of wires. I laughed it off and joked that I hadn't wanted to leave anything behind.

Miles of rusting train tracks stretched between us. She sent me a card with a cat on it that said, 'Good Luck!' in bubble letters. I stuck it up in my new room. The walls were the colour of seasickness. I stopped answering messages and spent weekends wandering around art galleries holding hands with boys who brought me sunflowers, while she sniffed powder off kitchen tables and shuffled to The Stone Roses across someone's stepdad's carpet. My boyfriend came to visit and he seemed small and vulnerable beneath the shiny new buildings. He raised his eyebrows at my long, black coat and drank too quickly around my new friends. He laughed at their names and their too-loud voices. I could see what he saw, but I didn't want to think about the ways in which I was different to them. We broke up over the phone as I sat in the bell tower of an old gothic library, running my fingers along the pages of leather-bound books. I bought a bike and got knocked off one night by the wing mirror of a passing car, while gazing drunkenly at the moon. Home seemed small and far away.

She studied Hairdressing at Newcastle College. She told me her lecturer said that coloured dye was 'passé'. I thought about her small hands as I backcombed my hair alone in my student room. She called me to tell me that she was dropping out of the course, but keeping the expensive products. I imagined her at her dressing table, skin damp beneath her pink bathrobe.

'It's okay for you,' she said. 'You've always known who you wanted to be.' I was working long nights in sweaty pubs, serving gin and tonics to bankers with ties around their heads and going to parties in old factories strung with disco balls. I was surviving on instant coffee and scrawling lecture notes in lip liner on scraps of paper, while everyone else typed diligently on their MacBooks. I thought that she was being unfair.

Missed birthdays and sour gossip lay strewn across the country. Muddled sentences detailing drunken trips to A&E and strange men in VIP areas leaked across my cracked computer screen. I heard she was going out with a bouncer with a scar across his face who could hold her whole bum in the palm of his hand. I worried about her, but I was busy learning how to pay a gas bill and roll my own cigarettes.

She sent me a message in the middle of the night.
'Something bad has happened,' it said. I typed a line of emojis from my phone at the bus stop as I made the dark

journey across the city home from work. I tried to imagine what kind of madcap situation she'd gotten herself into.

'It's really bad, Em,' she typed. I frowned as the little dots next to her name that meant she was writing flickered on and off.

'What is it?' The dots goaded me from the palm of my hand.

'I can't write it down.' I took the train straight home to her. We rode the bus through the sagging streets, weeds tumbling onto the motorway, just like the old days. She looked pale against the red and yellow squares of the seats. I asked her about it.

'Leave it, Em,' she said. 'I can't say it yet.'

We put on some sequins and lipstick in my old bedroom with Morrissey, trying our best to pretend that nothing was missing. The dirty bars that had once been delicious felt cold and plastic. Gotham had stopped serving trebles and the Dog & Parrot was stocked with fresh toilet roll and sold Espresso Martinis and truffle fries. We slipped between doorways trying not to notice. Closing time came and we blagged our way into the casino in Chinatown, with all the other people who didn't want to go home. They felt in their pockets for stray coins, panicking at the light of the morning beginning to drip through the window of the Gate. Boys with bullish faces glanced around the room, seeking us out. She breathed through her nose and looked at the table.

She told me about all of the times she had gone out without me, because I wasn't there. She told me that she felt strange in the clubs where women twirled on tables covered in feathers, but her new friends bought Grey Goose by the bottle, and besides, she didn't have anyone else to dance with. She told me that one night she met a student in the smoking area who wore white jeans and lit her cigarette with a silver Zippo. She said that he rolled his eyes through the smoke and said, 'Let's get out of here, shall we?'

He took her to a house party in Heaton where he mixed her a cocktail in the kitchen, then pressed her up against the wall and kissed her. She told me she liked it at first, but then everything grew confusing. The music sounded far away and the other people at the party melted into distant rooms. The student took her into a bedroom, and she felt scared and wanted to leave but he locked the door and wouldn't let her go. She stayed the night and the next morning she vomited all the way down the bus and everyone looked at her and nobody asked if she was okay.

I went to the bar and bought two glasses of white wine and a tube of salt and vinegar Pringles. I held her hand and we watched the people around us as they began to fray at the edges. We shared the back seat of a taxi and I saw her outline silhouetted against the window, as orange streetlamps sputtered in the first light of the morning.

I returned to my new life with a bright white sickness in my head. I knew that in my desperation to become someone different, I had left her behind. I turned my back on our half-cut world of drinking and dancing and dreaming of other places. I sat in expensive pubs and changed the texture of my vowels for women who did not wear makeup or drink pints of lager and were always warm enough. I imagined her smoking in a sequined dress in the queue outside of Digital. I wanted to climb back through the years and slip my arm through hers. I wanted to cut out the parts of myself that were selfish and rotten and wanted things that were bigger than us.

I sent her some Percy Pig sweets from M&S, and a postcard telling her I loved her because I didn't know what else to do. The parcel got lost in the post and she got taken to hospital in an ambulance with acute appendicitis. The doctors cut open her body and took bits of her out of it. She cried because she thought she wouldn't be able to wear a bikini again. I couldn't help but think that boy had left parts of himself lodged inside of her soft belly like shards of glass. I wished that I could offer her my own appendix as an apology, small and shiny and covered in blood.

# Duck Race

## Crista Ermiya

*Canard. Noun. An unfounded rumour or story. From the French, meaning duck or hoax.*

URBAN LEGEND SAYS JIMI Hendrix once busked on Chillingham Road. Elle Castellan likes to picture it, although she knows it's unlikely to be true. The story started to circulate in 2007 from an article in the *Chronicle*, 40 years after Hendrix supposedly strummed on one of Heaton's main streets. It's true Jimi Hendrix did come to Heaton, to stay overnight at Chas Chandler's mam's place on Second Avenue, opposite Elle's flat where the No. 1 bus stops. There's a plaque:

> Chas Chandler 1938–1996
> Founder member of the 'Animals'
> Manager of Jimi Hendrix & Slade
> Co-founder of Newcastle Arena
> Lived in this house 1938–1964.

Elle repeats the busking story as gospel when people come to stay. In 1967, Hendrix was on tour in the UK with Englebert Humperdinck (yes, really, Elle tells her sceptical listeners) and when it came to the Tyneside gig, Chandler put Jimi up at his mam's place. She points across the street to the plaque opposite the flat, offering it up as circumstantial evidence to her visitors this hot July weekend, Chuck and his seven-months pregnant wife Merel. Elle's only goal in life is to get through the weekend; to fulfil her duties as host, and then never have to think about the wretched pair ever again, beyond obligatory congratulations once the baby arrives. Ever since the visit was arranged, shortly after the New Year, Elle has been fantasising that it would be cancelled at the last moment; a non-fatal but absolutely urgent pregnancy emergency, like Kate Middleton's extreme morning sickness; or perhaps the sudden collapse of the airline they were taking from Rotterdam. She shouldn't have agreed to the visit, but July had seemed so far away. Now here it was, the days and months having crept forward with smug inevitability.

Elle searches for her keys. Chuck and Merel utter all the appropriate 'oohs' and 'wows' at the Hendrix story, although Merel mainly wants to get inside to use the toilet. Elle points her to the bathroom, through the kitchen at the back. It's a typical Tyneside flat, similar to the one Elle shared with Chuck in Jesmond, only this flat is smaller and the backyard is shared with the woman who lives in the flat upstairs. It's mostly their cats that share the space. The upstairs neighbour has three, Elle has one, a ginger tom called Triangle. All four are sitting outside on the concrete, studiously ignoring each other, grooming their arses, legs stuck up in the air or stretched out like rigor mortis in the sunshine.

Elle shows them the front bedroom where they'll be sleeping. 'Oh, what a lovely bed,' exclaims Merel. It's a black metal four-poster bed that Elle has had since Bristol. This and the piano were the only furniture she brought up with her when she came to Newcastle. Chuck has the grace to look embarrassed, although Elle had never quite caught them in the act. 'I've had it for years,' Elle tells Merel, and

Elle can see the exact moment on Merel's face when she remembers too. 'The mattress is new,' Elle adds. She gives them a brief tour of the rest of the flat: the hallway with its cupboard under the stairs of the flat above, and the little Alice in Wonderland door. 'Didn't we have one of these in Jesmond?' asks Chuck. 'The gas meter was there.' Elle nods.

'Isn't it sweet?' says Merel. 'It looks like something from a fairy tale.'

'It's where I keep Triangle's cat food and litter,' Elle says. She shows them the sitting room with the TV and piano, and her box room, which she grandly refers to as her studio, the floor space invisible under the airbed she'll be sleeping on for the duration of their visit. It's where Elle does all her work – 'I'm working on a series of poems based on the life of Jimi Hendrix,' she tells them – but mostly she uses the room for the work she actually gets paid for, editing articles for academic journals. 'Isn't that what you were doing in Bristol?' asks Chuck. 'I didn't know you'd gone back to that.'

At the turn of the millennium Elle had been working for the publishing department of a Learned Society in her hometown of Bristol. Chuck was a linguistics researcher at Newcastle University, where they had been building an electronic corpus of dialect speech in Tyneside. They met at a conference, where they discovered they were both poets. Or an aspiring poet, in Elle's case. Chuck had already had a respectable number of poems published in small press magazines and was putting together a chapbook. Elle's work was still stashed in notebooks under her bed. After several months of a cross-country relationship, largely facilitated by EasyJet's Newcastle to Bristol route, they decided that Elle would move to Newcastle. Elle couldn't remember how or when the decision had been made. One day it simply became accepted that she would be the one who moved. Chuck was tied to the University and it wouldn't be easy for him to find a comparable post in Bristol. The unspoken assumption was that Elle didn't have a career as such, so it would be easier for her to find work in other capacities.

'Yes, I've gone back to that,' Elle replies. 'It allows me to work from home.' Merel smiles kindly. 'It's so convenient, isn't it?' she agrees. 'I can't imagine having to work in an office.' Merel's fourth poetry collection is due out next Spring.

'You have such a cosy home,' Merel declares, once they're settled. 'I've never been a fan of homes that look as if no one lives there. This is very comfortable.' Elle has spent the best part of a month decluttering, tidying and cleaning, but now she understands she hasn't done a good enough job, nowhere near good enough. Elle is aware, from the endless photos on their various social media accounts, that Chuck and Merel's large apartment in Rotterdam is pristine, their furnishings tasteful mid-century modern, the books on their shelves arranged in size and colour like an artist's palette. It's still Merel's apartment, Elle thinks. Chuck just lives in it. Despite her clean-up, the corners of Elle's flat are still cluttered with the detritus of her life; books piled up in no discernible order, unsorted sheet music in towers on top of the piano, and the evidence of discarded hobbies everywhere: knotted bundles of wool with unpaired knitting needles sticking out at odd angles, an old laptop waiting for resurrection, kettlebells and yoga-mats, an old flower press.

Chuck notices her ukulele lying on top of the closed lid of the piano. 'I don't play the piano much these days, so I thought I'd try a new instrument,' Elle explains. 'Did you know Jimi Hendrix started off on the ukulele before he taught himself guitar?' The story spills out of her, how Jimi and his younger brother Leon had found a one-stringed ukulele in some garage rubbish, and Jimi had played around with it, tightening and loosening the string, experimenting with tension and position to eke out a tune. Elle lightly brushes her fingers over the ukulele's strings, an open A Minor 7 chord, as it lays flat on the piano, and dismisses their inevitable half-hearted requests to 'play us something'.

'Perhaps later,' she says.

★

The smell of stale coffee fills the flat. Elle had made the pot before going to meet them at the airport, not to drink but to try and mask the smell of cat. She offers to make some fresh.

'Oh, not for me, thank you,' Merel says.

'It's the caffeine,' explains Chuck. 'We're avoiding it because of the baby.'

'We?' asks Elle.

'Oh, well, in sympathy you know? It's the least I can do,' Chuck says.

'I do have some tea,' Elle offers, 'Yorkshire or Camomile?'

'Camomile would be lovely,' Merel accepts graciously. She arches a perfectly threaded eyebrow, 'Are you a royalist?'

'What?' Elle is taken aback, but then laughs with sudden understanding. 'Oh I see, the mugs.' Elle has an assortment of royal family commemorative mugs. 'No, but I think someone in Heaton must have been. I got these from one of the charity shops on Chilli Road, St Oswald's Hospice, I think. I'd been listening to "Anarchy in the UK" the morning I found them, and it seemed like a sign.' Merel sips her tea out of a silver jubilee mug and smiles blankly.

For several years there had been a souvenir photograph of Prince Charles and Lady Diana propped in the high window of a house on the corner of Warwick Street, the one where Diana is dressed in royal blue and wearing her sapphire engagement ring. It couldn't be seen from the ground, but the picture was in view of anyone who might be sat on the left-hand side of the top deck of the No. 1

after it turned from Heaton Park Road into Warwick Street to head into town. Elle didn't know how long it had been there. It was part of her mental map of Newcastle, one that was hard to share because it was made up of small things, the insignificant landmarks of the everyday: a ghost sign on an empty shop; a sycamore sapling springing up behind an old BT box; a black and white cat that sat in a particular downstairs window, and always turned its head at the same angle as she walked past; a window full of fat cactuses, some of them brown and turning to cork. And then one day on the bus Elle realised, with a pang, that the Charles and Diana picture had gone, and she couldn't say for certain whether it had only just gone, or if she just hadn't noticed until now. And then she found the mugs in the St Oswald's shop.

'Actually, that gives me an idea for lunch,' Elle says. 'We could go to The Wild Trapeze on Heaton Road. It's not far from here. The owner of the café is an artist and he's painted a picture of Prince Philip in the nude. It's hanging over the inside of the doorway.' Merel looks horrified. 'The queen is fully dressed,' Elle reassures her.

The weather apps all predict that the sunshine will hold for the weekend and Elle suggests they go for a walk in the parks first, if that's okay with Merel: Heaton Park, Armstrong Park, Jesmond Dene. Elle hadn't visited the Dene much when she and Chuck lived in Jesmond; their flat was slightly too far away from it and much closer to the town moor. At the time she had preferred the grassy moor wide open to the sky, with its improbable population of grazing cows in the middle of a city. Jesmond Dene was all trees and shadows and made her feel claustrophobic. But after Chuck had left for Merel and Rotterdam, she moved to Heaton, and it felt to Elle that the green spaces had opened up to her. Instead of closing in on her like a trap, the trees were now a comfort, and she walked through one or other of the parks almost daily, navigating her loss beneath great lime and oak and poplar, past the civic splendour of the flower borders by the pavilion in Heaton Park, and through the wild garlic in Armstrong Park, the endless rhododendron and ferns. Birds sang. It was as if their volume suddenly turned up as soon as Elle walked through the park gates. Once, near the bird feeders in Armstrong Park, Elle had heard with a thrill the drumming of a woodpecker, its tattoo an erratic heartbeat in the hidden spaces above her.

Their walk is aimless and leisurely with no goal in mind, only one foot in front of the other, over and over. Admittedly, Elle finds it quite pleasant to walk with companions for once, in the sunshine, dodging the fat bees that buzzed drowsily in their path. She suggests walking on to Pets Corner but Chuck vetoes the idea, saying it isn't a good idea for Merel to be so close to livestock, the goats and the Soay sheep and the pigs, so they turn back, returning via the shoe tree.

'Ah, I've heard of this,' Merel exclaims. 'It's the tree in Julia Darling's novel, isn't it?'

'*The Taxi Driver's Daughter*,' Elle confirms.

'That's it,' Merel says. 'It came out the same week I arrived in Newcastle.' It's a subtle stab. Elle had been working in the English Department as one of the undergraduate admin support staff when Merel had been named the North Eastern Literary Fellow and came to take up the post. It's where Merel had met both Chuck and Elle. Elle has heard from mutual acquaintances in the department that the couple have been back to Newcastle several times in the intervening years, but since the wedding, she hasn't faced them until this weekend.

They gaze up. Over time, the shoe tree has grown into 'trees', plural. Boots, trainers, shoes of all sizes are hung at various heights by their laces on at least three different trees. 'They look too heavy for the branches,' Merel observes. 'Yes, I suppose so,' says Elle. 'Students add to them when they're leaving. It's hard work though. I once saw three students trying to land a pair of walking boots up there. I'd walked to Pets Corner and when I came back an hour later they were still at it.'

'And why do they do this?' Merel asks.

'I don't know,' Elle admits, 'A sign that they were once here?' She pauses, then says, 'It's a reminder that Newcastle was their home.'

They go straight from the park gates on Heaton Road down to The Wild Trapeze. 'You weren't lying about the painting,' Chuck says inside, marvelling at the picture above the door. The queen is dressed in royal blue and laughing good-naturedly, sitting by a Hockney-esque swimming pool in a yellow chair. In the foreground, a naked Prince Philip has his hands clutched strategically over his crown jewels. Three corgis line up in the background. On the counter are postcards of the painting for sale. Chuck buys one, 'For my office,' he tells Merel. They order the all-day breakfasts, one full English, one vegetarian and one vegan, although none of them is vegan. 'I have to manage my weight while I'm pregnant,' Merel says, while Elle adds brown sauce to her full English. 'Of course,' she murmurs. They eat under the restaurateur's paintings that line one red wall: portraits and self-portraits; idiosyncratic yet easily recognisable versions of 19th century paintings by the pre-Raphaelites; *Beata Beatrix*, Dante's lost love. Elle has a local history book at home, *Heaton: from Farms to Foundries* by Alan Morgan, and in it, there's a photograph from the 19th century of a class of school children. One of the teachers looks exactly like the painter and café owner, and Elle likes to believe it really is him, that he has been here forever in various guises.

'This is a lovely place,' Merel concedes. They turn to discussion of the food in Rotterdam. The city has such a vibrant culture, Chuck and Merel inform Elle, several times. 'We have a very big street market in Rotterdam, one of the biggest in Europe,' Merel says. 'Chuck and I often go there for waffles, but it's very diverse, you can get so many different things. Sometimes we get Turkish pizza, don't we?' Chuck gives a non-committal nod and takes a sip of the coffee he has ordered. 'Sounds great,' Elle says, girding herself against any continued rhapsody about their vibrant, diverse city. But Elle's tone must have given her away, because Merel changes tack and instead mentions how difficult it is to keep her weight down during the pregnancy when there is such tempting food everywhere. 'I noticed that there were a few takeaways on Chillingham Road. Do you eat from them very often?'

'Sometimes,' Elle replies shortly. There had been that awkward moment on the journey back to Elle's flat after she had gone to meet Chuck and Merel at the airport, when someone had tried to offer Elle a seat on the Metro thinking she was the one who was pregnant. She laughed it off, feigning indifference, and offered the seat to Merel in turn, who almost refused it – 'I'm pregnant, not decrepit', she had later complained – but the air in the Metro carriage was hot, even with the breeze from the open windows, and Elle could see that Merel's feet were swelling slightly in her ballet flats. Merel eventually took the seat and Elle stood, swaying next to the baggage between herself and Chuck.

As they eat within sight of the naked Prince Philip, music spools out from unseen speakers and Elle recognises its familiar pulse: 'House Burning Down' from Hendrix's *Electric Ladyland*. It was during the recording of this album that Jimi and Chas Chandler had parted ways. In her first years in Heaton, Elle had read with sympathy Jimi's accounts of meeting Chas and moving to England. Chas had struck Jimi as 'a pretty sincere guy' and Jimi didn't feel particularly rooted in the US anyway. There'd been a letter from Jimi in New York to his father in 1965 that Elle had particularly taken to heart: *I still have my guitar and amp, and as long as I have that, no fool can keep me from living.* He was himself, wherever he happened to be. Elle is about to draw their attention to the song before the DJ on the radio starts to talk over the end, but Chuck and Merel are idly bickering over the misremembered location of a curry house in Fenham, where Merel had lived during her time in Newcastle, and so Elle says nothing.

★

*Seventh Annual Cluny Duck Race.*
*All proceeds in support of Ouseburn Farm.*
*Ducks are on sale from The Cluny @ £3 each. Prizes for*
*1st & 2nd place in the race, and for Best Dressed Duck.*
*Best Dressed Judging: from 2.30pm*
*Duck Race: 4pm*
*Strictly one duck per entrant. Ducks may be*
*decorated/dressed up, but nothing to aid speed or direction.*
*No sails, motors or jetpacks!*

The next day they walk down to the Ouseburn through the streets of Mowbray and Hotspur, passing front yards growing wild with yellow Welsh poppies, lavender, and buddleia. Heat shimmers up from dusty cars. Behind Warwick Stadium park, they negotiate the steep slope down to the arches of the railway viaduct. The plaintive baas of sheep follow them down, their woolly bodies packing up against fences in the distance, jostling to get fed by small children holding their hands out flat. Chuck starts to fuss but Merel snaps that she isn't planning to get licked by any sheep and they fall into an awkward silence. Elle buys the ducks (numbered 263, 264 and 265) and Chuck buys the drinks, and they sit outside on the small square of green with their plastic cups.

Merel announces she's getting bored with pub life. There's only so much soft drink she can imbibe, and she is spending half her weekend peeing. Chuck and Elle wait for her outside on the green as she goes to the toilet again. Over the chatter of people with beers comes a voice, 'Chuck!' and they both turn to see Jack, a playwright who teaches on the MA at Northumbria University. He bounds up to them, making no attempt to conceal the curiosity on his face at seeing the two of them together. 'Hey man, are you back? I heard you were coming to take up a post at Teesside, but I thought that wasn't until the New Year.'

'Chuck and Merel are both staying with me before Chuck's readings in Middlesbrough,' Elle says carefully, to stall any misunderstanding.

'Oh, the festival? Yes that. But what about the lectureship?' Elle is puzzled and Chuck coughs. 'Oh, nothing's finalised.'

'Ah right,' Jack says. 'I must have heard the wrong rumour. So, you're staying for a few days? Look, I've got to rush but I'm doing something at Alphabetti next week if you want to meet up for a pint.'

'I'll be in Middlesbrough and Stockton most of next week, but I'll see what I can do,' Chuck says unconvincingly. Jack looks back at where a woman is waiting for him on the pavement outside 36 Lime Street Studios. Elle recognises her as an artist who specialises in creating work from objects found in the Tyne. She waves. Elle waves back. 'Yeah, that'd be great, no pressure. I'll send you a message.' Jack turns to Elle, appraising her networking potential. 'You too, Elle. It'd be good to catch up,' he says blandly.

'Sure,' Elle says, and he lopes back to the artist. Elle turns to look at Chuck and is going to ask about the lectureship, but she sees Merel returning, so instead says, 'The race is going to start soon. We can wait over there by the finish line.'

They wait on the river path opposite The Cluny. A barman has strapped on some waders and is standing in the Ouseburn with a long-handled fishing net. Some of the regulars shout at him, 'Looking sexy there' and he gives a long-suffering thumbs up. He's also thrown what looks like a tennis net across the width of the river to serve both as a finishing line and to stop 300 rubber ducks floating off to the North Sea. At one point a real duck swims up, and he raises the net to let it through to cheers from the crowd. The river isn't exactly gushing in the dry summer so it's going to be a while before the first rubber ducks come into view. Merel goes back inside the pub with a poet acquaintance they've bumped into, waving Chuck away. 'You stay here with Elle,' she commands. 'I know you'll want to see who comes first.' She turns to Elle. 'He's so competitive.'

While they wait at the finishing line, Elle asks Chuck something that has been nagging at the back of her mind all weekend. She says, slowly, 'Chuck, when you called to ask if you and Merel could stay this weekend, did you know then that Merel was pregnant?'

'To be honest, I didn't think you'd pick up the phone,' Chuck replies.

Elle still doesn't know why she had answered the phone that day. Her anxiety whenever the phone rang had been an ongoing irritation for Chuck when they were together. If the landline rang and Chuck was in the bathroom or the kitchen, Elle would sit there frozen until whoever was calling rang off, or until Chuck broke off from whatever he was doing to come and answer it. If he'd been in the bathroom, he'd eventually come out of the shower or the toilet and ask 'Who was it?', and she would have to admit, yet again, that she didn't know, and sit there while he shouted at her: 'What if it was my parents? What if it was an emergency?'

'Did you know?' Elle repeats. Chuck looks away, pretending to scan for ducks, and says, 'I wanted to talk to you.'

He had babbled, inconsequentially, minor gossip about the poetry scene in Rotterdam, while she remained silent on the other end of the line. Elle wondered now if this was because he hadn't known what to say. What could he say, the burden of the baby clagging his tongue? Eventually, Chuck had asked if he and Merel could come and stay in the summer, just for a weekend. He was coming to the North East for a series of poetry events and it would be great to catch up, the three of them. Elle had heard herself say, 'Yes, of course,' and that was that.

Chuck turns back to her. 'You look softer now, less angled. It's nice,' he says quietly. He looks at the curve of her stomach over her jeans and Elle instinctively crosses her hands over her body. Over the past decade, as her weight crept up, Elle had often wondered if this was what she would have looked like if she had carried their baby to term. It was disconcerting to see the same thought go through Chuck's mind.

'Merel seems very happy in Rotterdam,' Elle ventures. 'Would she be interested in moving if you got a job back here?'

Chuck lightly touches Elle's hands, still crossed over her torso. She almost succeeds in not flinching. He quickly lets go and shoves his hands into his pockets. 'There's no need to mention our conversation with Jack to Merel,' he says. 'He got the wrong end of the stick.'

The first ducks finally come into view. A couple of front runners get caught in some eddies and start travelling sideways, then backwards. The crowd groans, as does the Cluny barman, who has been standing in the water for the best part of an hour waiting to net the winner and the second prize. A third duck breaks away from the pack, falls on its side, and bobs on the water with tortuous slowness. Eventually, to the sound of 'come on, come on' from the onlookers, it reaches the finish. The barman scoops it up with his net and pulls it out, hands it to a young woman in a Cluny T-shirt who holds it aloft like the torch on the Statue of Liberty. She shouts out a number, but Elle can't hear it. 'What did she say?' A man next to her says, 'I think it was 265'.

Chuck thumps Elle on the arm. 'Wait, isn't that one of ours?' he asks. It is. It's Elle's. They had to provide a name and telephone number for each one, and Elle had given Merel and Chuck's names first, 263, 264, and her name last, duck 265. Chuck waves wildly at the young woman. 'It's ours, that's ours! 265!'

The young woman shakes her head and tries to tell them something, but Chuck is already pushing Elle along the path and over the footbridge, then back round to the sloping bank, past an old wooden boat stranded in the mud.

'Did you say 265?' Elle asks tentatively, and Chuck pushes her forward to stake her claim. Elle can't be sure afterwards whether Chuck did it on purpose, but the mud is deeper than it looks, and the soles of her trainers have no purchase on the slope. Elle slips, and her whole body slides into the mud, her hands pushing furrows as she flails to stop herself. She hears Chuck laugh behind her. Everyone on the footbridge, and on the river path, is looking at her. The barman has waded out of the water and offers Elle a hand up. 'It's usually me that does that,' he says. 'Are you okay?' asks the young woman. 'Oh, yes,' Elle lies, 'I'm fine.'

'Is that 265?' she asks. The woman pulls a grimace as she looks back down at the winning duck. 'It's 165,' she says. 'I'm really sorry'.

'Oh god, it's not your fault. This sort of thing always happens to me. I should have known.' Elle smiles and shrugs her shoulders. She squelches back to Chuck. 'What did she say? Did you win?' Elle explains the mix-up with the numbers. 'Only you, Elle. That can only happen to you.' Elle wonders if he's going to apologise for shoving her forwards, but all he does is hand her back her half-empty plastic cup of beer, grown warm in the sun. She necks it.

Merel and her friend come out to look for them. 'What happened to you?' she asks in surprise. Before Elle can say anything, Chuck says, 'Elle thought she'd won the duck race and fell over in her rush to claim the prize. But it was the wrong number, of course.' Merel's friend laughs but Merel appears genuinely solicitous. 'How awful for you, Elle. Do you need to clean up?' Elle raises her hands. 'I'll just rinse my hands for now, the rest will have to wait until I get home.' She goes back to the river, not sliding this time, and tries to rinse her hands in the water. She's only partly successful. The mud is stubbornly stuck to her hands, and Elle wonders how clean the Ouseburn is anyway. She walks back to the others, shaking her hands dry. 'I'm all pubbed out', Merel declares. 'Why don't we just go back now and Elle can have a shower and change?' She kisses her friend goodbye. The friend gives Elle a pitying smile and a nod to Chuck. 'Shall we get a cab back?' Chuck asks. 'I can order an Uber. If you're tired you probably don't want to walk back up the hill,' he says to Merel. 'I don't think I can get into a taxi. I'd get the seats all muddy,' Elle says. 'Oh, of course. Shall we just meet you back at the flat then?' Chuck says.

'Don't be ridiculous,' Merel rebukes him. 'We can all walk back together.'

They walk slowly, and bits of mud drop off Elle's jeans as it dries and cracks in the sunshine. Chuck googles the water quality of the Ouseburn on his smartphone, pulls a face and says, 'Sometimes it's best not to look these things up.' Elle hears a click behind her. 'Have you just taken a photo?' she asks.

'Chuck,' Merel reprimands him, 'Don't be so immature.'

'I'm not a child,' he says peevishly, and Elle senses this is an old argument, unresolved.

At home, Elle showers and gets dressed. She's not sure what to do with her muddy clothes, as she's worried the mud will clog up the washing machine, so she pegs them outside on the plastic washing line, thinking she'll beat the mud off later. Chuck laughs. 'You're the only person I know who'd hang dirty clothes out to dry.' There's a graze on her hand that she hadn't noticed before. Merel produces a fresh tube of antiseptic cream from her wash bag, and dabs some on gently. The feeling of Merel's fingers on her palm is soothing. 'Thank you,' Elle says.

Maybe it's the heat, but the three of them are lethargic, slouched in Elle's sitting room with no intention of going out for their last evening. Elle finger picks 'All Along The Watchtower' for them on her ukulele, but her grazed hand makes it hard to exert the right pressure on the frets and the sound comes out as a series of plinks. 'Hendrix would be proud,' Chuck says and Elle smiles faintly. They spend the evening binge-watching a series on Netflix. Halfway through, Elle remembers the ducks. 'Oh, we forgot to collect them after the race.' She starts to cry, but doesn't know why, so she pretends to blow her nose and gets up to go to the toilet. She knows they'll have been picked up in the net, but for nights afterwards, she will keep dreaming that their rubber ducks are bobbing along the Ouseburn to the Tyne, then out to the

North Sea, their small bodies vanishing underneath the great vastness of the sky.

That night, the cats are all howling in the back yard, Triangle in some kind of stand-off with the cats from upstairs. Elle listens to their strange mewling from the box room, their cry like the sound of abandoned babies.

Elle stares up at her studio ceiling in the dark. She hadn't asked Chuck how he felt about becoming a father. She was sure now that he had never told Merel about her miscarriage. They hadn't told anyone. Sometimes, when she lay on her back, like now, she flashed back to the RVI. She'd lain down on her back on the examining table for the 12-week ultrasound, and had stared at the large empty sac on the screen above her. 'I don't understand,' Elle kept saying. 'I can't see anything.' The nurse had to ask her to keep quiet while she took some measurements on her screen. She'd then taken a breath and gently explained to Elle that sometimes when the foetus doesn't develop properly, the body doesn't always recognise this straight away. The pregnancy hormones don't drop and the pregnancy appears to continue as normal, sometimes for weeks afterwards. They recorded it as a missed miscarriage. It was like the worst sort of practical joke, her own body conspiring with the universe to produce this awful hoax. Elle started bleeding that evening. It was as if now she had been let in on the joke, there was no point in her body keeping up the charade, and it began to let go. She bled for weeks. There was one very bad night, and then the rest of it was simply a kind of seeping while she went about her daily business: working, answering emails, grocery shopping, cooking. Pretending to be normal.

Now it's Monday morning and Elle isn't sure who is more relieved. She accompanies Chuck and Merel to Central Station, where they are booked on a train to Middlesbrough.

They travel to the station by taxi and Elle waves them through the ticket gates, after an awkward kiss on the cheek from Chuck, and a warm hug over her bump from Merel. Elle returns home on the No. 1, sitting on a front seat on the top deck. On the other front seat is a dad with his little boy, who is pretending to drive the bus, vroom, vroom, vroom. Elle listens to the boy while she watches the people on the pavements below. The bus snakes its way up Grainger Street and Pilgrim Street, past the Laing Gallery and the City Library on John Dobson Street, skirting Sandyford and Shieldfield on its way to Heaton. Elle gets off the bus and takes out the keys for her front door. She glances at the plaque across the street and pictures Jimi Hendrix standing on Second Avenue, a stranger, his guitar strapped over his back like home.

# Loftboy

## Chrissie Glazebrook

WHAT I SAW THAT night, it was a flat-out shocker. Course, even if I was busting to tell someone, I can't, because I should never have been there. If anyone finds out, *bam*! Polis, the wrath of God, the Ukrainian Folk Dance Society – they'll all be descending on our house. I've already been hit by a plague of boils.

To stretch a short story long, it all kicked off when the man from the housing association turned up. This guy had no neck, a cold sore at the corner of his mouth and tufty eyebrows like hamsters' nests. But he was wearing a suit, which in my mother's eyes made him a bit of a catch, so she invited him in.

'Coffee, Mr...? Sorry, I didn't catch your name.'

'Johnson,' he said. 'Barry Johnson.'

Her face hit the floor like a dropped pie. Maybe she'd been hoping for something more exotic, a Quentin or a Dominic, a Hugh or a Tristram. I struggled to keep the smirk off my mouth.

'Heather Boot,' she said, recovering, fluffing up her hair, wiping her hand on her jeans. I was half-expecting her to curtsey. She pretended to search inside the cupboard. Sauce bottles clinked. Packet soups slid in an avalanche on to the worktop. 'Do you mind instant? We seem to be all out of Blue Mountain.' Right, like she ever buys anything but Café Instanto from Kwik Save.

'That'll do fine,' he said, grinning and winking at me. Either he was humouring her because he knew she was trying to impress him or he's into fifteen-year-old boys. Tell you what, if he fancies his chances with me, he'll be packing his theodolite into an arse-shaped holder.

'So, what is it you're up to, Barry?' simpered Mum, handing him a mug advertising tranquillisers, a gift from the doctor's surgery to one of their best customers. 'To what do we owe this honour?'

He took a slurp of coffee, grimacing. 'I'm giving the houses in the Terrace the once-over on behalf of the housing association,' he explained. 'In case you or any of the other tenants wish to exercise your right to buy.'

A snort shot down my nose. If anyone was loco enough to want to buy one of these slums, they'd already be in a mental home. Mum impaled me with a warning glare.

'Homework, Billy,' she snapped.

'Done it.' She'd make me pay for this later.

Mum turned back to the surveyor, pressing him. 'And would you say they're in good nick?'

Johnson considered his words. 'They're not too bad,' he said. 'For their age.' Translated, this meant *Let's see how you feel when you're a hundred and five years old.*

She sat opposite him at the kitchen table fluttering her lashes, making her cow's eyes dance in an attempt to look alluring; an obscenity coming from someone with a face like a bucket of frogs. How could she show herself up like this, flirting with a guy with *herpes*! My own mum, shagsake! When I caught her eye, she jerked her head towards the ceiling, meaning *Bog off up to your room*. Naturally, I ignored her and stuck my nose in the free newspaper, pretending to read the sports pages.

Johnson must have got a degree in boring. He droned on about eaves and cornices, fascias and soffits, about attic vents, cornerstones, bearing walls and collar beams. After an earful of this, Mum decided to give up on sparkling. She tapped her foot under the table, willing him to finish his coffee and just *go*.

'They don't build houses like this anymore,' said No-Neck, a dreamy expression on his face. He was probably reminiscing about medieval buildings with lancet windows, straw instead of carpets and a fowl roasting on an open fire in the middle of the floor, like we saw on a school trip to Bede's World.

'That's a relief.' Mum, deadpan, forced out the words through clenched teeth.

'For a kick-off, it'd be illegal nowadays.'

My ears pricked up. *Illegal*. That was an exciting word, like *sex*. I watched all the true crime programmes on TV, and American cop shows, sometimes even Brit stuff like *The Bill*. I was kind of fascinated by life on the wrong side of the law. It sounded a real turn-on, like a foreign country full of drug-smugglers, people-traffickers and money-launderers strutting around in designer gear, wearing shades all the time, with mobile phones clamped to their lugholes. I wouldn't mind visiting there one day. Maybe.

'The roof space has no dividing walls,' Johnson continued. 'No demarcation between one house and the next. There's just one huge attic running the whole length of the terrace. A paradise for burglars.' He tugged a handful of eyebrow and cast a yearning gaze at the biscuit tin.

Mum's eyes glazed over. It was clear she wanted rid of him. Out came the cherry-flavoured lip balm. She dipped her finger in the pot, smeared some grease on her gob and practised her pout in the mirror.

'I don't wish to seem rude, Barry, but I need to get to the library before it closes.'

Huh? Where did that come from? There wasn't a single, solitary book in this house, unless you counted her mail-order catalogue. I doubt the lying cow knew where the library was, never mind its opening hours.

Johnson nodded, sank his coffee and shambled to the door. His jacket looked at least one size too small for him. Maybe he bought it from the charity shop, a dead man's suit. 'Thanks for the, er, the coffee,' he said. 'Bye then.'

Rigid with disappointment, Mum couldn't bring herself to answer, just shut the door behind him, then turned on me.

'What are *you* gawping at, face-ache?' she snapped.

I shrugged my shoulders and slunk off to my room for a think.

The houses where we live in Skinner Terrace used to be miners' cottages, in the olden days when there used to be coal. Now the Elswick Housing Association owns them and rents them out to people down on their luck, or on benefits, or too bone-idle to get jobs. Dirt-poor people like me and Mum. White trash, though trash of any colour can apply, even mixed-race trash like me. The buildings are crumbling, made of ancient red brick, and they don't have front gardens like proper houses, just a patch of scrubby grass the size of a postage stamp or the odd dying bush for the local dogs to use as a lavatory, and back yards where the wifies hang out the washing and park the wheelie bins. There's zero view apart from a row of identical houses opposite. Gazers, that's how I think of them, because that's all they're good for, standing and gazing at each other across a narrow path. Skinner Terrace is a pedestrianised area, which means the alley isn't wide enough for cars to drive along. There's a back lane with a takeaway pizza parlour at one end belting stinky steam-grease through the ventilation, and a chop suey place at the other. The housing association did up the houses on the cheap, turning tiny box rooms into bathrooms for pygmies, poisoning the rats and sealing their bolt-holes, fixing air bricks so that we won't die from fumes while we sleep.

Misfits Avenue, that's what it ought to be called. Deadbeats Road. Lepers Lane.

One thing you can say about Skinner Terrace, it has its share of cultural diversity, if culture's the word. To the left of us, there's this old Ukrainian bloke, Mr Joblonski, who lives on his own. Even though he used to have a wife, Mum's gut instinct warns her he's a kiddy-diddler, though that's probably more to do with her xenophobia and believing all the rabble-rousing crap she reads in the tabloids. She's ordered me never to go into his house, not even if he offers to show me some puppies, and says I mustn't look him in the eye in case he takes it as some kind of come-on. On the other side are Mr and Mrs Nazir, a decrepit old couple whose house stinks of spicy food. They have floods of visitors, dark-skinned young men who I reckon must be family but naturally, Mum suspects they're druggies who come to fix up at the Nose Hairs' crystal meth laboratory in the cellar, so I'm not allowed to speak to them either. Don't get the idea that Mum's a racist or anything, but it's hard not to see a pattern emerging, as in *Steer Clear of Foreigners: Paedos and Peddlers, the lot of 'em*. Anyone who's not a Newcastle purebred, who wasn't born within the sound of Armstrong's hooter, is bound to be dodgy and best avoided, goes the word according to Heather Boot. That includes me, the fruit of her own womb, fifty per cent Geordie, fifty per cent Mauritian on my father's side. Dual heritage. Mixed race. Or half-caste, as she so sensitively puts it.

So that's us, the tenants from Hades, the residents of Skinner Terrace, low-rent homes for the terminally hopeless.

A row of houses with one thing in common: a joined-up attic that runs above them.

I can't wait to explore it.

Mum was banging about in her bedroom like a herd of stampeding buffalo. She sounded mad as all hell but don't ask me why. Maybe it was because she got suckered in by Barry Johnson, thinking she'd found herself a potential love match then realising he was just a dweeb in a bad suit. She was getting ready to go to her spiritualist meeting at Jubilation Hall, to spend an evening communicating with the dead, when she could do that from the comfort of her own sofa just by watching *EastEnders* on the telly.

She galumphed downstairs, then slipped into her slingbacks and clacked through the hall, poking dents in the laminate flooring. I tiptoed to my bedroom door and spied on her titivating herself in the mirror, zhushing up her hair and pulling faces at herself. She'd dressed in a tartan mini skirt and a lowcut top that flashed her cleavage – well, as long as she hitched up her bra so tight that her nips were practically at ear-level. It must have been simpler to raise the Mary Rose. Who did she see staring back at her? Pamela Anderson? Paris Hilton? If so, her self-image was seriously out of whack. The Wicked Witch of the West End, more like.

Without so much as a 'See ya' or 'Laters', she was off out the door, tappy-lappy down the front path, to her date with the dead. Whoo! Now was my chance to check out that communal attic.

Standing on the upstairs landing, I stared at the wooden hatch in the ceiling, the portal to the mysterious place in the roof. Stared and stared until my neck ached and I could see ants crawling in the corners of my eyes. Me, I'm not the type to rush things, so I ripped a page out of the message pad by the phone and made a list of the things I'd need.

# LOFTBOY

*Ladder*
*Torch*
*~~Ballaclarva~~ Ski Mask*
*Gloves*

The thought of entering the secret world upstairs excited me, made me twitch inside my pants, but also frightened me. What if my body got stuck in the hatch? The opening wasn't all that big, but then again, I'm not exactly built like a wrestler either. Into my mind flashed this picture of myself wedged halfway in and halfway out, legs dingle-dangling, feet kicking out into nothingness, while the top part of me, my head and arms, were stuck in the creepy darkness above. My body was jammed tight in the hole, unable to move in either direction, like a jumbo sausage in a tampon tube. Even though I was the skinniest person in the known universe, I'd probably swell up and die from panic, knowing my luck. Mum would come home from a night communing with the departed to find my lifeless body swinging from a hole in the ceiling, and *then* there'd be trouble.

No, it was too, too scary. I had to think about it, consider all the angles. I liked to be thorough. Failing to plan means planning to fail. Mrs Doig, our PSE teacher, told us that.

Years passed. OK, I'd thunk. Now I raced around finding the gear from my list. I dressed, as best I could given the materials, like a SAS operative. On went my ski mask, only because it was so ancient and shrunken from a zillion washes, it was tight as a vice and made my head hurt. I hoped it wouldn't stop the blood getting to my brain. Mum's yellow Marigolds, the rubber gloves she used for washing-up, weren't exactly SWAT team quality but they pulled way up over my wrists so at least they'd be spiderproof. I took the stepladder out of the airing cupboard where it was stashed between half-used pots of paint, and placed it directly beneath the hatch. Finally, I checked that the flashlight was working and jammed it in the pocket of my trackie bottoms.

Legs and arms trembling, I placed my foot on the first rickety step and hoovered in a deep lungful of air, trying to calm myself. Then on to the second step, and the third, and again, on to the top rung. The aluminium ladder wobbled beneath me as I reached up and slid back the hatch leading to the attic. Courage, don't lose it now, Billy. What was the worst that could happen? A fally-off accident, maybe a few bruises, a dented ego, who would know? Breathe, man, don't forget to breathe.

Lift-off! Taking the weight on my arms I heaved myself into the roof space, then flopped down on the dusty boards, panting like I'd just done a cross-country run. I shone the torch around me. What a sight! It was like an alien landscape from another planet, weird and almost beautiful in a way. Hey, get me. Cue swirly music. The furry lagging spread over the floor to keep the heat in reminded me of something I'd seen once on telly, deep underwater shots of the wreck of the Titanic, eerie and otherworldly. But where the liner reeked of richness, the material in the attic looked slapdash, eked out, smacking of builders' yards and job-lot cheapness.

All around me ancient lumber was stored: a scraggy artificial Christmas tree and a plastic bag spilling over with decorations; half-used rolls of wallpaper, an old exercise bike, an umbrella for a patio table, and, sprawling flat out, as though it had collapsed after just running a marathon, a coat-stand made of twisted metal, shaped like a very tall, emaciated person. And boxes, mountains of cardboard boxes that had once contained shoes, a camping stove, bottles of Mexican beer, beaded car seat covers, a satellite mini-dish. A pile of bin liners, stuffed full of who-knows-what, was stacked at one side of the hatch.

So I sat there, quaking with nerves, heart pounding,

getting used to my new surroundings, gazing at the Boot family chuck-outs, wondering why the idea of recycling seemed to have passed my mother by, until I decided to check out the rest of the communal attic space. I rolled up the ski mask as it was squinching my head, and crawled on my knees across the floor, shining the torch in front of me, until I reached the entrance to the house next door. This wasn't something I was looking forward to. It was old man Joblonski's place, and he wasn't exactly known to be houseproud, not since his wife died. OK then, he was a hobo, a filthy nobchunk, and you wouldn't risk eating or drinking anything from his house in case you caught the Black Death or something. Frig knows how he managed to survive. His immune system must have been on constant overtime fighting off all those bacteria and superbugs.

I struggled through the opening, trying to breathe through my mouth to stop myself being gassed by the pong. What a tip! Spiders were the last thing you'd need to worry about in this attic; there'd be mice, rats maybe, or feral cats, rabid wolverines, scorpions, rattlesnakes, all kinds of deadly, plague-carrying wildlife like that. Even the air in there felt wrong, thick and offensive and dangerous to breathe, as though it could turn to sludge in your throat and suffocate the life out of your body. A mountain of plastic bin liners faced me, a shiny black Everest of I-daren't-think-what, corpses of long-dead pets maybe, hacked-off limbs of door-to-door salesmen, the boiled head of a rent collector. Grisly.

I didn't intend to hang around, never meant to stay and explore, but something seemed to draw me like iron filings to a magnet. Nebbiness is my failing, curiosity my seventh deadly sin. It's what killed the damn cat, and it nearly finished me off too.

Positioning myself above the hatch, I managed to grasp it by the edge. My fingers, turned by nerves into sausages, fumbled with the wood. It was jammed tight, swollen with damp. I managed to ease it until, millimetre by millimetre, it surrendered. My heart boomed in my ribcage. I forgot to breathe. Almost wetting myself with excitement and terror, I jerked the hatch to one side. There, beneath me, was Mr Joblonski's flat.

Once I'd regained my puff, once my pulse stopped throbbing in my neck, once my eyeballs returned to their sockets, once the groan of floorboards settled, I listened. My ears strained with the effort. Nothing. Only silence. Then it dawned on me. Wednesday evening was Jobba's regular visit to the Ukrainian Club, a prefab building on Westgate Road tucked between the adult movie shop and a fishing tackle emporium.

Empty. The flat was empty. Just time for a quick skeg round, see if the old bugger had owt interesting.

Boom-di-boom-di-boom, thudded my ticker as I eased myself down through the hatch onto his landing. He had a chair directly below the opening, a huge leather monstrosity like the one at the dentists. Balancing my feet on the arms, I crouched to a sitting position and listened again. Silence. Complete, velvety silence.

The whole place reeked of cabbage, as if they'd slapped it on the walls instead of paint. Cabbage, tobacco, and a fusty smell like mouldy laundry. Not a good combo. I stared at the threadbare carpet. It stank like a damp dog. I felt sick. A quick in-and-out, that was as much as my nose could take.

In the living room, among the clutter of prehistoric furniture, was probably the oldest telly in the world. It wouldn't have looked out of place on the Antiques Roadshow. Jobba existed in a foreign timewarp light years away from normal humans. Bet he'd never even heard of DVDs or iPods, never mind McDonalds.

The place was creeping me out. I felt as if I'd stumbled into Dracula's castle, or another dimension, one inhabited by super-skunks, a world where Airwick hadn't been invented.

Before hauling myself back into the loft, I decided to take a peek in the bedroom. Don't ask me why. I wish to God I'd never done it.

The door was slightly open, revealing a dark, old-fashioned wardrobe with an oval mirror mired beneath layers of dust. On top of the bed was not a duvet, but a shiny red quilt that could have doubled as a coffin lining. Dozens of religious icons decorated the walls, illustrations of shifty-looking saints and Baby Jesus in his incarnation as a bonobo chimp. What a frigging dump.

It was while I was clocking the pictures that I heard it.

A snort. Not a snore. A snort, like people make when they rouse unexpectedly. Or die suddenly.

I froze. Maybe I wet myself a tiny bit. I was *terrified*, remember.

Slouched in a basket chair on the far side of the bed was – what? Who? Jobba, old Mr Joblonski, resident of Elswick, formerly Odessa. He was almost unrecognisable.

His wife's wig, the hideous one she wore after her hair fell out, adorned his head. It had slipped, come askew. Synthetic blonde curls cascaded over his forehead, covering one eye. He resembled the spawn of the Elephant Man and Lily Savage.

I realised that he was breathing deeply, a wheezy croak in his throat as if he was practising his death rattle. Mr Joblonski was not dead, but asleep. Although every instinct screamed to get the fuck out of there, I was paralysed, mesmerised, traumatised. I crept towards him until I was so close that I could smell his earwax. I noticed a single hair on his bulbous nose end, fine and kinked like a stray pube. He must have nodded off, slumped in his chair like a badly packed parcel, in his blonde wig and borrowed clothes.

Mr Joblonski was dressed in his dead wife's dressing gown, a turquoise velour number with poppies embroidered on the collar.

In his left hand, a framed photograph of their wedding day had almost slithered from his grip.

Between the fingers of his other hand a raw, veiny chipolata dangled limply.

My throat snapped shut with shock. I loathed myself for having discovered Mr Joblonski in this most private moment. If I could have undone the dead – the *deed*; if I hadn't been tempted into breaking and entering – well, *entering*; if I could have turned back the cock – the *clock*; believe me, I would have.

'I'm famished, get us some supper, you useless bell-end.' That was Mum's greeting when she returned from Jubilation Hall.

My legs were still shaky. The crotch of my jeans felt damp with sweat or something. My hair smelled of cabbage. Tiny blood vessels kept popping behind my eyes.

'What do you fancy?' My voice came out all jittery.

'Microwave us a couple of those mini whosits,' she hollered. 'You know – Kievs, whatever they're called.'

Suddenly I found myself sobbing.

# Ekow on Town Moor

## Degna Stone

EKOW FELT SAFE ON the town moor. It was the only place where he could unload the clutter of his mind, the only place keeping him sane when all he wanted was to sink into nothing and let life wash over him. He never really understood why, but whenever he saw the cattle that grazed there, he felt centred. When he was a teen, it had always been the place he went when he felt an argument brewing with his mum. It was just the two of them, Ekow's dad had died before he was old enough to have any real memories of him, and when things got too tense, the moor was where he headed.

It was easy enough to avoid people on the moor. It was so vast, it never seemed like there were more than a dozen people on it at any one time, except on a Saturday morning when Park Runners gathered at the Exhibition Park end. This morning, he left his basement flat early to warm up around the boating lake in front of Wylam Brewery. Mist settled on his cropped afro in tiny crystals as he jogged along, his lungs slowly easing into a rhythm and his hips loosening up. His mum would walk him home through this park after school when the brewery was still the derelict military vehicle museum. There were no swans then, and no herons, but they still brought handfuls of oats to feed to the few ducks that swam there, and he would tell her about his day: how he wasn't sure if Fin was still his friend because he hadn't sat with him that lunchtime, or that Shanaz hadn't invited him to her birthday party and the rest of the class seemed to be going. She always listened and made sympathetic noises but never tried to fix whatever was broken. She would often just say, 'Let's see how things are tomorrow, no need to worry about what is in the past.' As he got older, he noticed that she never seemed to live in the past. She never talked about her life before his dad had died, or gave much away about her childhood. She said that dwelling on things was a waste of time, better to focus on what is happening now before it's gone. That wasn't the trouble he had been facing these past few months. He couldn't keep himself in the present, but it wasn't the past he was afraid of. Instead, it was that every moment might be a springboard to thoughts of a future that he couldn't control.

He picked up speed and powered through the swing gate onto the moor. The dew on the ryegrass seeped through the fabric tops of his running shoes, but he didn't notice. Soon it would feel like he'd left Newcastle behind completely. He'd learned to ignore the constant drone of traffic from the central motorway over the years, and instead focused on the calls of the wrens and the meadow pipits that he could never quite see.

He ran steadily up one of the hills he used to sledge down with friends on the rare occasions that it snowed. He could feel the cold October air beginning to claw at his lungs as he slowed down toward the top of the hill, trying to catch his breath. From here he felt like he could shrink the whole of Newcastle until it fitted into the palm of his hand and pocket it. It was the only place he felt his life had any meaning. He looked all around waiting to see if anyone was close so that he might open his mouth as wide as he could and scream. He wanted to listen to the sound of his own sorrow disappear as it got swallowed up by the mist. Something was holding him back though. He'd grown into the sort of man that it was easy to miss in a crowd. He barely took up any room and when he spoke, you would have to lean in to catch what he was saying, only to find that you'd forget what he had said as soon as someone else spoke. His mum was the only person who saw him differently, who didn't see his gentleness as a weakness. She'd once told him that he was an old soul, that when she looked into his eyes, the world seemed to make a little more sense. After his dad had died, she hadn't stopped living but Ekow had become her world, and now that was slipping away from both of them.

He looked around until he could see which part of the moor the cattle were grazing on; they never seemed to be in the same place twice. They brought the moor back to life when they returned at the start of each spring. His mum was scared of them, especially when they ventured too close. He could never reassure her that they wouldn't trample her to death. She always said it'd be just her luck if she was the first person to cause a deadly stampede. It amused her that his favourite place was the one that didn't feel like you were in the city at all. She felt he was trying to find something that he hoped would be out on the moor. And she was right: there he found that it didn't matter if no one ever noticed him. When he was as close to the middle of nowhere as Newcastle can get, he felt like he was enough. He didn't have to feel uncomfortable in his inability to impress other people.

It always came as a surprise to Ekow when the cows disappeared at the end of November. He tried not to think of where they went to, but he knew most wouldn't be back the next year. When the cattle moved on, the town moor was a desolate place, and this year he knew that she would be gone too.

He loved the cows though, the way they ignored the mayhem of The Hoppings when it rolled onto the moor in June. Their general indifference to human activity made him smile. This was the first year they had missed The Hoppings. Ever since he was tiny she'd taken him; she loved the noise of it and the way it stretched as far as you could see, a gaudy, overpriced city where you paid to terrify yourself on the fastest, highest rides. She loved the excitement of it. They had been every year of his life. Even when he got older and only wanted to go with his friends, she'd insist that he go with her, too. She loved to tease him about the first time he went on the big waltzers when he should have stuck with the teacups. A young guy had taken the sign that read 'Scream if you wanna go faster!' too literally, and kept spinning Ekow round and round as he screamed that he wanted to get off. His mum wanted to give that guy such a piece of her mind, but Ekow was mortified and just wanted to leave. She'd had to hold on to him as his head kept spinning, steadying him all the way home. The wind cut through him deeply now, and the ground drained the energy from his legs as he ran on.

These days he always felt less sure-footed. He was trying to run the fear and tension away, but he just seemed to be winding himself up further. He could feel himself hurtling back to the time his husband had left him. Ekow was a homebody: he'd been content to live quietly in Jesmond, but his husband had ambition and wanted more from life. They were opposites and this was the beauty of their marriage, although his husband had a hardness that Ekow had at first mistaken for strength. It always seemed to bring them to a place where Ekow felt that his heart would break. His husband hadn't understood what it really meant to be with someone who struggled to fill the space the world had made for him. When he finally became exhausted by the demands of living with someone so fragile, he gave up.

After that, Ekow started drinking every night to the point where he would pass out to silence the noise in his head, and though he tried to hide the fact that he was losing control from his mum, she knew he needed her. She'd insisted on having a set of keys to his small flat and one afternoon she'd found him passed out on the filthy kitchen floor. As the sound of her voice began to filter through the fog of what would soon become a disgusting hangover, he began to open his eyes. From that perfect vantage point, he could see the layers of dirt and the ossified morsels of food that had dropped under the cooker and been forgotten.

She'd cleaned him up, blitzed the flat and listened as he cried his heart out. 'You know, Ekow, I prayed for the world to stop when your father died. I don't even believe in God, but I prayed anyway. I wanted everything to end so that I wouldn't have to deal with the grief. But every morning there you were, needing something, needing everything from me. There were times when I'd drop you off at nursery and imagine not returning at the end of the day. But I carried on. I had to. I guess it was easier for me though. I had you.'

She had a habit of making everything alright. No matter how catastrophic things seemed, she could always help him to see a way out. 'Look around Ekow. There is beauty everywhere. Remember that, even when the darkness surrounding you makes it hard to see. You need to find something Ekow. You need a reason to stop yourself slipping away.'

He thought he'd found something running on the moor. The presence of the cows always seemed to signify that all was right with the world: that as long as cattle roamed on the town moor, nothing truly bad could happen. But the trees at the edge of the moor were catching autumn in their leaves, and every second took him further and further away from the point where they'd had all the time in the world. Every step reminded him that she was dying. He wanted to rage, but who was he angry at? Four weeks at the start of June had turned into four months and he knew he should be grateful, but every day he saw the look of fear and helplessness in her eyes deepen. Every day he felt grief swelling inside him. He wanted time to stop, to keep her alive.

She was his storehouse: the place he went to replenish his reserves. She held what was left of his mind together and he could sense the burden of it weighing on her shoulders. He had wanted to be the one to lift it from her but he didn't have the strength. It would be easier to let himself fall apart again.

Last night Ekow had left the hospice while his mum lay in that strange sleep that wasn't really sleep, where her face still held the tension of the pain she never complained about. He hated leaving her when death was so close, hated the thought that she would never breathe the air on the moor again and could only watch the weather through closed windows, guessing at the temperature outside. Sometimes she would send him out just to feel the weather on his skin when he returned. When he kissed her goodbye, she felt cold despite the warmth of the room. These days the air around her body always seemed two degrees colder. When she found the energy to joke, she'd say that she radiated a chill to keep everyone else at a distance, because no one knew how to behave well with the dying.

The mist should have cleared by now but instead had turned into thick fog, and the city had almost disappeared from view. It was time to head home. He ran down the hill barely keeping his balance. He pushed harder until his heart started thumping against his ribs and it felt like it would burst. He wanted to keep running, didn't want to return to his flat, didn't want to go back to the hospice because he didn't know what would face him when he did.

Without his mum to anchor him, he was losing any idea he ever had of himself, and with it his sense of who he was in this city. Newcastle was small enough to know every single street as well as you knew the rooms in your home but, as his mum began to drift away from him, he could feel himself getting lost. Without her as his guide, he had already begun to hover at the edges and, despite what she'd always tried to instil in him, he did not have anything saved for hard times. She was the one who kept him straight, helped him back on his feet back into work, helped him believe in himself.

'You need a goal Ekow, something to focus on. Keep your body active to still your mind. Keep running. Why don't you do the Great North Run? Or at least stop avoiding the Park Run. Maybe you'll meet someone there.'

He could hear the noise of the traffic getting closer as he ran toward the crossing at the Blue House roundabout. Though he could barely see them, he could just make out a line of cattle standing shoulder to shoulder, watching him. He wasn't disorientated by their closeness or the lack of visibility. He liked the feeling of being in a suspended state of time, like nothing else existed. The weak sun gave the moor a surreal yellow tinge. He'd been trying to prepare himself for what lay ahead, but he was scared. He used to know how to stop his thoughts from spiralling out of control, but now he needed to stop them from coming in the first place. He tried to hold onto the belief that for most people, feeling the urge to run into traffic was the mind's way of making sure that you didn't. Without his mum, he wasn't sure if he was most people.

He slowed down and focused on steadying his heart as his breathing returned to normal. He passed a young woman with a small child; Ekow recognised the logo on the boy's book bag, they were heading to his old school. He wanted to cry but he knew that if he did, he wouldn't be able to stop.

He couldn't hear the smaller birds above the noise of the traffic now, but he knew they were still there. With the solitude of the moor behind him, he listened to the rattle of a magpie and could just make out the shape of a crow on top of the traffic lights. It called out just as the lights turned red. They were more robust than the delicate birds who stayed mostly out of sight on the moor. The noise and busyness of the city didn't trouble them. Ekow knew he would have to adapt. He had to let his mum know that he would be alright, that he would be safe. He would keep his body active to still his mind. All he needed was the sanctuary of the town moor and her memory to keep him company.

# About the Contributors

**Jessica Andrews** writes fiction and poetry. She grew up in Sunderland and has spent time living in Santa Cruz, Paris, Donegal, Barcelona and London. She has been published by *The Guardian, Stylist, The Independent, Elle, AnOther, Somesuch Stories, Caught by the River* and Papaya Press, among others. She teaches Literature and Creative Writing classes and co-runs literary magazine, *The Grapevine*, which aims to give a platform to under-represented writers. Her debut novel, *Saltwater*, was published by Sceptre to much acclaim in 2019.

**Julia Darling** began her career as a full-time novelist, playwright and poet in 1987. She won the Northern Rock Foundation writers award in 2003, and was the Royal Literary Fund Fellow at Newcastle University. Her highly acclaimed novel, *The Taxi Driver's Daughter*, was longlisted for the 2003 Booker Prize and was shortlisted for the Society of Author's 2004 Encore Award. Her other writing includes the novel *Crocodile Soup* longlisted for the Orange Prize for Fiction and republished in 2015 by Mayfly, several collections of poetry and short stories, and numerous plays for stage, TV and radio. She was working on a new novel, *A Cure for Dying*, when she passed away in April 2005.

**Crista Ermiya** is a short story writer. Her debut collection *The Weather in Kansas* was published by Red Squirrel Press in 2015

## ABOUT THE CONTRIBUTORS

and was chosen by New Writing North as a 'Read Regional' title. Her story '1977' featured in *Best British Short Stories 2016* (Salt, 2016). She is a freelance writer and editor, and is an editorial assistant for the academic journal *Landscape Research*. Originally from London, of Filipino and Turkish-Cypriot parentage, Crista lives in Newcastle with her husband and son.

The late **Chrissie Glazebrook** was a comic novelist based in Newcastle upon Tyne. Her novels include *The Madolescents* and *Blue Spark Sisters*.

**J. A. Mensah** is a writer based in the north east of England. She has written for theatre with a focus on human rights narratives and the testimonies of survivors. Her first novel, *Castles from Cobwebs*, won the inaugural NorthBound Book Award and will be published by Saraband.

**Sean O'Brien** is a poet, critic, editor, translator, playwright, broadcaster and novelist. His poetry has won multiple awards, including the T. S. Eliot Prize, the Forward Prize (three times), and the E. M. Forster Award. His second novel, *Once Again Assembled Here*, was published in 2016, as was *Hammersmith*, a chapbook of poetry and photographs. His ninth collection of poetry, *Europa,* was published in 2018, as well as his second collection of short stories from Comma Press, *Quartier Perdu*. Born in London, Sean O'Brien grew up in Hull and now lives in Newcastle upon Tyne. He is Professor of Creative Writing at Newcastle University, and a Fellow of the Royal Society of Literature.

**Angela Readman's** short stories have won the Costa Short Story Award, The Mslexia Fiction Competition, and The Anton Chekhov Award for Short Fiction. Her debut collection *Don't Try This at Home* was published by And Other

## ABOUT THE CONTRIBUTORS

Stories in 2015. It won The Rubery Book Prize and was shortlisted in the Edge Hill Short Story Prize in 2015. She also writes poetry, and her collection *The Book of Tides* was published by Nine Arches in 2016. *Something Like Breathing*, her first novel, was published by And Other Stories in 2019.

**Glynis Reed** is a mother of two and lives on the North East coast. Glynis completed her MA in Creative Writing at Newcastle University. In 2007, she was awarded the Andrea Badenoch Fiction Award. She has been published in various magazines and was mentored by the novelist, David Almond. Glynis is currently working on a novel.

Originally from the Midlands, **Degna Stone** is now based in Tyne and Wear. She is a co-founder and former Managing Editor of *Butcher's Dog* poetry magazine, a Contributing Editor at *The Rialto*, and a Poetry Book Society Pamphlet selector. She received a Northern Writers Award in 2015, holds an MA in Creative Writing from Newcastle University, and is an associate artist with The Poetry Exchange. She is a fellow of The Complete Works III and received a Hawthornden Fellowship in 2019. Her latest pamphlet *Handling Stolen Goods* is available from Peepal Tree Press. 'Ekow on Town Moor' is her first published short story.

Recently retired senior lecturer in prose and scriptwriting at Newcastle University, **Margaret Wilkinson's** radio dramas have been broadcast on the BBC Radio 4 Afternoon Play; Saturday Drama; Writing the Century; and Woman's Hour Serials. She has also written two novels, many short stories. several short and full-length stage plays and film scripts. For many years she has contributed regular columns to the writing magazine, *Mslexia*, reviewing recent collections of short stories and disseminating ideas about prose writing through exercises and techniques she has developed.

## ALSO AVAILABLE IN THIS SERIES

*The Book of Birmingham*
Edited by Khavita Bhanot

*The Book of Cairo*
Edited by Raph Cormack

*The Book of Dhaka*
Edited by Arunava Sinha & Pushpita Alam

*The Book of Gaza*
Edited by Atef Abu Saif

*The Book of Havana*
Edited by Orsola Casagrande

*The Book of Tehran*
Edited by Fereshteh Ahmadi

*The Book of Istanbul*
Edited by Jim Hinks & Gul Turner

*The Book of Khartoum*
Edited by Raph Cormack & Max Shmookler

*The Book of Leeds*
Edited by Tom Palmer & Maria Crossan

*The Book of Liverpool*
Edited by Maria Crossan & Eleanor Rees

*The Book of Riga*
Edited by Becca Parkinson & Eva Eglaja-Kristsone

*The Book of Rio*
Edited by Toni Marques & Katie Slade

*The Book of Sheffield*
Edited by Catherine Taylor

*The Book of Tbilisi*
Edited by Becca Parkinson & Gvantsa Jobava

*The Book of Tokyo*
Edited by Jim Hinks, Masashi Matsuie
& Michael Emmerich

ALSO AVAILABLE IN THIS SERIES

# The Book of Sheffield
*Edited by Catherine Taylor*

Known for both its industrial roots and arboreal abundance, Sheffield has always been a city of two halves. From elegant parks and gardens to brutalist high-rise estates and the hinterland nightclubs of 'Centertainment', it is a city caught between the forges of the past and the melting pot of the present.

Bringing together new short stories from some of the city's most celebrated writers, The Book of Sheffield traces the contours of this complex landscape from both sides of the economic dividing line. From the aspirations of young creatives, ultimately driven to leave, to the more immediate demands of refugees, scrap metal collectors, and student radicals, these stories offer ten different look-out points from which to gaze down on the ever-changing face of the 'Steel City'.

*Featuring: Margaret Drabble, Tim Etchells, Naomi Frisby, Philip Hensher, Helen Mort, Geoff Nicholson, Gregory Norminton, Johny Pitts, Désirée Reynolds & Karl Riordan*

ISBN: 978-1-91097-437-7
£9.99

ALSO AVAILABLE IN THIS SERIES

# The Book of Birmingham
*Edited by Kavita Bhanot*

'Each story provides its own rich, textured, and complex history of the city post-WWII to the present.'
– *Rewrite London*

Few cities have undergone such a radical transformation over the last few decades as Birmingham. Culturally and architecturally, it has been in a state of perpetual flux and regeneration, with new communities moving in, then out, and iconic post-war landmarks making way for brighter-coloured, 21st century flourishes. Much like the city itself, the characters in the stories gathered here are often living through moments of profound change, closing in on a personal or societal turning point, that carries as much threat as it does promise.

Set against key moments of history – from Malcolm X's visit to Smethwick in 1965, to the Handsworth riots two decades later, from the demise of the city's manufacturing in the 70s and 80s, to the ongoing tensions between communities in recent years – these stories celebrate the cultural dynamism that makes this complex, often divided 'second city' far more than just the sum of its parts.

*Featuring: Balvinder Banga, Alan Beard, Jendella Benson, Kit de Waal, Sharon Duggal, Joel Lane, Malachi McIntosh, Bobby Nayyar, C.D. Rose & Sibyl Ruth*

ISBN: 978-1-91097-437-7
£9.99

ALSO AVAILABLE IN THIS SERIES

# The Book of Liverpool
*Edited by Maria Crossan & Eleanor Rees*

A baby blown out of an upstairs window by a WWII bomb lives to hear others tell the tale...

A woman embarks on a long-term obsession with a city landmark, abandoning her lover for the Liver...

A bricklayer working on the foundations of a never-built cathedral becomes its evangelist, its full splendour soaring only in his mind...

Bringing together fiction from some of the city's most celebrated writers, *The Book of Liverpool* traces the unique contours that decades of social and economic change can impress on a city. Set against key historical moments from the Second World War to the Capital of Culture year, these stories question what 'belonging' and 'home' mean in the Liverpudlian context, from the regenerated city centre to satellite suburbs, from the sparring cathedrals to the no-go concrete housing estates. Liverpool emerges in these short stories as a city in constant flux: haunted by ghosts, buoyed up by myths, and shifting with an ebb and flow like the Mersey itself.

*Featuring: Dinesh Allirajah, Tracy Aston, Beryl Bainbridge, Clive Barker, Ramsey Campbell, Frank Cottrell Boyce, Paul Farley, James Friel, Margaret Murphy & Brian Patten*

ISBN: 978-1-90558-309-6
£9.99